LP F McH
C.
Mc ☑ **W9-BBM-389**

The dropped living room

2001.　　**HA**

CASS COUNTY PUBLIC LIBRARY
400 E. MECHANIC
HARRISONVILLE, MO 64701

The Dropped Living Room

Also by Frances Y. McHugh
in Large Print:

Emerald Mountain
High on a Hill
The Hyacinth Spell
The Rocking Chair
Shadow Acres
Window on the Seine

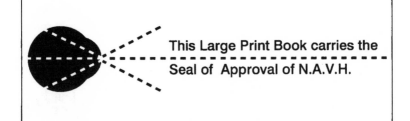

This Large Print Book carries the
Seal of Approval of N.A.V.H.

The Dropped Living Room

Frances Y. McHugh

0 0022 0080793 7

Thorndike Press • Waterville, Maine

CASS COUNTY PUBLIC LIBRARY
400 E. MECHANIC
HARRISONVILLE, MO 64701

© Copyright 1971, by Lenox Hill Press

All rights reserved.

Published in 2001 by arrangement with Maureen Moran Agency.

Thorndike Press Large Print Candlelight Series.

The tree indicium is a trademark of Thorndike Press.

The text of this Large Print edition is unabridged.
Other aspects of the book may vary from the original edition.

Set in 16 pt. Plantin by Myrna S. Raven.

Printed in the United States on permanent paper.

Library of Congress Cataloging-in-Publication Data

McHugh, Frances Y.
    The dropped living room / by Frances Y. McHugh.
        p. cm.
    ISBN 0-7862-3468-7 (lg. print : hc : alk. paper)
    1. Divorced women — Fiction. 2. New York (N.Y.) —
Fiction. 3. Large type books. I. Title.

PS3563.C3685 D7 2001
    813′.54—dc21   2001027761

THE DROPPED LIVING ROOM

Chapter One

I'd loved our brownstone house on East 78th Street ever since Jack and I had moved into it just after we were married. But beginning with that gruesome day last February, I decided the whole atmosphere of the place had changed, and one never knew what was going to happen in it next.

Our block was mostly brownstone houses, which were privately owned and well kept. People had bought and remodeled most of them, as we had ours, for the sake of having a modicum of suburban living in the midst of the urban chaos known as New York City. The windows of the houses were clean, the curtains expensive, and many people had made an attempt to beautify the façades with window boxes and the areaways with boxed and potted bushes and shrubs, which in the summer bloomed and brought a breath of country to what would otherwise have been a drab city block. Even on that bleak and fateful February day, some of the shrubs, which were evergreens, softened the stone faces of the buildings and made one feel that somewhere, some place, there was the promise of another spring.

I hate February in New York, and this day was typical: cold and windy. As I was on my way home, about five o'clock, it began to rain and freeze. Dusk had descended almost without my noticing it, and when I did I quickened my steps.

Boy, my large tan mastiff, was straining at his leash, and with the glassy street I was having trouble staying on my feet. Then, to make matters worse, a cat streaked out of an areaway, and Boy made a lunge for it. I felt myself slipping and struggled to keep from falling. Fortunately, a man, passing me just at that moment, grabbed my arm and saved me from a bad fall. With one hand holding me up, the other hand pulling Boy's leash to keep him from trying to follow the cat, who had slunk beneath a parked car, he was, to say the least, a godsend.

For a moment I couldn't get breath enough even to say, "Thank you," but at last I did and said, "Thank you very much. I'd have fallen if it hadn't been for you." I looked up at the man then and saw he was young, dark and handsome. In spite of myself, I smiled. But I pulled my arm free from his grasp and started walking away from him. However, in my high-heeled shoes, without overshoes or storm boots, I discovered that when I'd slipped I'd done some-thing to my right ankle. The man, seeing I was having difficulty, grabbed me again, this time putting an arm around me. "Take it easy there," he cautioned.

This embarrassed me, and I gave a ner-vous little laugh. "I seem to have wrenched my ankle," I said apologetically. I looked up at him again and discovered his eyes were a warm brown, large and kindly. He said, "Perhaps I'd better help you to your home?" There was a strength about him that I needed at the moment, and I was glad to lean on it.

Maybe I shouldn't have, but I said, "Oh, if you would. I live just a few houses up the block. Could I hold onto your arm, if it wouldn't be too much trouble?"

"No trouble at all," he assured me. "As a matter of fact, I've dreamed about things like this, but nothing so wonderful has ever happened to me before." His voice was deep and pleasant.

Again I looked up at him, this time to see if he was joking. He was. He grinned like a silly schoolboy, showing straight white teeth, and said, "It isn't every day I get a chance to help a beautiful damsel in dis-tress." I smiled, and we walked slowly to-ward my house.

When we reached the brownstone steps that led up to my front door, I stopped. "This is where I live," I said. "You've been very kind. Thank you again."

But the man kept hold of me. "I'd better help you up the steps," he said, and proceeded to do so. At the top of the steps, Boy began tugging at his leash, anxious to get in out of the cold, now that he had lost interest in the cat, and my rescuer had to help me control him. Gratefully I accepted his aid until we were safely in the vestibule, then I said, "Well, thank you again." I had the strangest feeling that when we parted, I would be losing a friend. Which showed the emotional upset I was in that afternoon.

The man raised his hat and bowed. "It was a pleasure," he assured me. I noticed he had brown hair with a slight wave. It was cut quite short. He didn't turn away, and I began to unlock the front door with the key I'd taken from my purse. The man was scratching Boy's ears and talking to him, and Boy looked at him gratefully as if to say, "Thank you."

Just as I opened the front door, the man took a pack of cigarettes from a coat pocket, then started to search for a match. After a moment of fruitless searching, he asked, "You wouldn't have a match, would you?"

I said, "I'm afraid I haven't one with me, but if you will come in, there are some in the living room."

He smiled, and something happened to my heart; something that hadn't happened to it in a couple of years. "If you don't mind?" he said.

I leaned down, unsnapped Boy's leash from his collar and told him, "Go up to Ronny, Boy," and the dog loped up the stairs, leaving me alone with the strange man. He was standing respectfully waiting for me to lead the way into the living room, which was to the right of the front door as one went in and down two steps. A wrought-iron railing at either side of the steps made part of the hall a sort of balcony to the living room. It was the type of room the real estate agents designate as a dropped living room.

The man closed the front door behind us and followed me. Out of the corner of my eye, I could see him glancing around the room. Jack's picture in a silver frame was on a table, and the man casually sauntered over to it and picked it up, asking, "Your husband?"

I could feel my lips tighten. "He used to be," I said quickly. "We're divorced now." I could feel a pulse begin to throb in my throat as I slipped off my beaver coat, put it on a chair and put my matching Cossack-type hat on top of it. Then I picked up a pack of matches from the glass-topped mahogany coffee table, which was in front of a sofa, struck a light and held it for my visitor to light his cigarette. I hoped he wasn't noticing how my hand was trembling as he bent near me to touch his cigarette to the match flame. Any mention of Jack always upset me — even now, and especially that day.

The man said, "Thank you," and replaced Jack's picture on the table. I guess I gave a sigh when the picture was safely back on the table. I hadn't liked having it disturbed. But of course my visitor didn't know that, and he'd really been very kind, so I said, "Won't you sit down a moment? Perhaps you'd like some sherry before you go. It's cold outside."

He smiled gratefully. "Thank you. I'd like some very much. But can't I get it? Your ankle — ?"

I sank down on the sofa beside the cheerfully crackling fire which we always kept burning on cold days. "My ankle *is* beginning to ache a little," I had to admit. Then I noticed he was fingering his hat. It was a brown felt and looked new. "Just put your hat and coat on that other chair beside the

12

steps," I told him. So he took off his over-coat, which was also brown, and put it on the chair which backed up to the railing beside the two steps to the hall. Then he laid his hat on top of it.

I said, "There's a closet in the hall just beneath the stairs, to your left as you go along the hall toward the back. It was originally a clothes closet. But Jack — I mean Mr. Evers; he was my husband — had it made into a bar just after we bought this house. When you open the door, a ceiling light will go on, so you will be able to see. Everything is in the closet: sherry, glasses, a tray. Or if you'd rather have a highball or something on the rocks, you'll find a choice of rye, Scotch or bourbon, and there's a small electric refrigerator with ice cubes."

He smiled down at me, and I couldn't tell whether my cheeks were feeling warm from the glow of the log fire or because of the way he was looking at me. "Sherry will be fine," he said. "And don't worry about me finding the right door. My friends say all they have to do is blindfold me and turn me loose, and instinctively I'll head for the nearest bottle of liquor."

I had to laugh. "Or the nearest woman?" I teased.

He grinned at me over his shoulder as he

went up the two steps from the living room and into the long, narrow hallway. "Unh, unh," he said, "the women always find me first."

Whether he was kidding or serious, I had to laugh again. There was something very nice about him, and he was certainly very gentlemanly.

I leaned my head back on the sofa as I waited for him and glanced around my living room. I'd seen it hundreds of times, probably thousands, but I found myself wondering what this strange man thought of it, seeing it for the first time. I'd always felt it had a comfortable look that few rooms achieve. There were two windows at the front facing the street, the kind that run from close to the floor nearly to the ceiling. I'd had Venetian blinds made for them, and dull gold drapes to hang at the sides of the windows. The sofa I was sitting on was covered with a soft green material.

On the opposite side of the room from the steps up to the hall there was the fireplace. The sofa on which I was sitting came out from the side of the fireplace, while the other side was flanked by a large wing chair, upholstered in cherry brocade. Jack used to like to sit in that chair and smoke his pipe. He'd looked very nice in it. He was the long, lanky type with straight blond hair parted on the side and light brown eyes flecked with yellow. But to get back to the room: the walls were just off white, the floor covered with an apple green broadloom.

At the opposite end of the room from the front windows, bookcases framed a wide doorway through which could be seen a room I used as a sitting room. It was up two steps, making it level with the hall.

The furniture in both rooms was mostly mahogany, of the Colonial period, and there were always magazines scattered everywhere, no matter how hard I tried to keep them picked up.

I'd almost forgotten the man in the hall until I heard a dull thud that brought me back from my daydreaming and my memories. The entire room always brought back memories of Jack more than any other part of the house.

The noise in the hall startled me, and I sat up straight, calling, "What was that?" Then, not waiting for an answer, I got up and limped to the railing so I could see into the back of the hall.

When I saw what it was, I stifled a scream. Lying on the floor, a knife sticking in his back, was Jack. He had on a tan tweed suit, and there was a stream of blood on the jacket. I put the back of my hand over my mouth to stifle another scream; I knew my eyes must be wide with fright and horror.

My visitor knelt beside the body of my dead ex-husband and turned it so he could see his face; then a groan escaped him, as if the dead man were someone he knew and loved. He felt of the body and tried to find a pulse in one limp wrist. But evidently there was none, so he got to his feet, came to me and led me back to the sofa. Then he returned to the hall closet and came back with a bottle of rye and two glasses. I knew he would have had to step over Jack's body to get them and realized it must have been unpleasant for him.

I covered my face with my hands, hot tears dropped from between my fingers, and my shoulders shook with silent sobs. I had loved Jack very much and still missed him.

The man poured rye into a glass. The bottle clinked against it, and the thought went through my mind that his hand must be trembling. He put the bottle on the coffee table and sat down beside me, saying, "Here, drink this." But I kept on crying silently. I couldn't stop.

Then he put an arm about my shaking shoulders. "Poor darling," he said huskily. His sympathy broke the dam. I turned to him and buried my face on his shoulder, and the silent sobs became audible, choking, hopeless.

He held me close and let me cry. After a while I stopped, lifted my head and pulled away from him. I knew my face was wet and blotchy and I must look awful. But I didn't care.

The man held the glass to my lips and made me drink. Then he took a drink himself. For what seemed like an eternity we sat and stared at each other blankly. Then, drawing in a deep shuddering breath, I asked, "He was dead?"

The man nodded, took my hands in his and held them tightly. "When did you see him last?" he asked.

I was tense, scarcely breathing. "You know who he is?"

He nodded. "The picture," he said. Then he waited for me to answer his question. I said, "I saw him this afternoon, about three o'clock. He telephoned me earlier and said he wanted to see Ronny. That's our son. He's four. It was the first time I'd seen Jack since he went down to South America on an engineering job two years ago. Everything else — I mean the divorce — was arranged by mail and phone. But I had agreed he could see Ronny several times a year. This

17

was the first time he'd asked to, although he's been back for several months."

The man gripped my hands hard. "When you were out with the dog, was he here?"

"Yes. He was here when I left. He came about three, and I went right out. I stayed out until I felt sure he was gone. I didn't want to have to talk to him. I left him with Ronny. Althea was here, too. She's the maid. I've had her ever since I was married — six years. Before that she worked for my mother."

There was a sound on the stairs. It was Ronny. Plaintively he called, "Mommy."

I started, and I and my visitor looked in the direction of the voice. We could see part of the stairs from the living room, and peering through the uprights of the banister was my small son. His curly red hair was mussed, and his big blue eyes were heavy with sleep. He was wearing a one-piece sleeping garment with feet attached to the pants. It was almost the same blue as his eyes. His chubby cheeks were flushed with recent sleep, and in one arm he clutched his favorite toy, a rather dilapidated-looking panda.

I gripped the hands of the man beside me, thinking, Oh, dear God, what shall I do about *him?* Aloud I said, "It's Ronny, my son. He's been sick today. A slight cold. I kept him in bed after his nap this afternoon. I didn't want his father to take him out."

The man gave my clutching hands an answering pressure, and we both must have had the same thought: Could the child see the body of his father lying in the hall?

Finally the man said, "Take him back to bed, and I'll call the proper people."

I gasped. "Oh, *must* you?" Instantly I had visions of police swarming all over the place and newspaper headlines.

"You know I must," the man said. "There's no other way." He was tall and broad-shouldered, and I had the feeling he could be depended upon to do the right thing at all times.

I pulled my hands from him and stood up. "All right," I said. "I'll call Althea to stay with Ronny so he won't come downstairs again." Then I hesitated. "But she's down in the kitchen preparing dinner. The kitchen and dining room are downstairs, and she'd have to come up and pass through the hall to get here. Maybe she shouldn't see — ?"

"See what, Mommy?" Ronny asked.

"Nothing, dear," I told him quickly.

It was a problem. There didn't seem to be any answer to it. If I went outside and summoned Althea to the basement door, which

19

was just beneath the flight of brownstone steps that led up to the front door, and brought her upstairs from the outside, she would see Jack's body the minute she entered the front door. So that wouldn't help any.

I stared at the man beside me, momentarily baffled. He said, "You take the boy upstairs and stay with him. I'll hold the fort down here."

I gave him what I hoped was a grateful look and limped out of the room. Instantly he was beside me. "Your ankle," he said.

But I waved him aside. "I can manage," I told him. "It isn't bad now." I started up the stairs, shoving Ronny before me. "Back to bed with you now," I said as sternly as I could, my knees feeling weak and empty.

"But I don't want to go to bed," Ronny whimpered. "I haven't got any more sleep."

I said, "Ssshhh! Scoot now. Hurry up."

Climbing the stairs ahead of me, he asked, "Who is that man?"

"A friend of mine."

"What's his name?"

That I couldn't answer, because I didn't know.

Over my shoulder I called, "There's a phone in that back room — on the desk."

Chapter Two

When I finally had put Ronny in bed, I suddenly realized I'd left Sylvia's letter on the desk in the sitting room. And the phone that strange man would have to use to call the police was on that desk. I could remember the letter word for word, and I didn't want anyone to see it; not the strange man who had been so kind to me and certainly not the police. The letter read:

My dear Mrs. Evers:

You will no doubt be surprised to hear from me. And I must say it took me a long time to get up enough courage to write you. You probably won't believe it, but I felt a little guilty about taking your husband away from you, because I know how I would have felt if someone had taken mine away from me, back in the days when I still loved him. My first husband, I mean. Because I still love Jack and always will, and I think I'd kill anyone who tried to take him away from me.

But I didn't start this letter to tell you how

much I love Jack. I am writing to you because I must see you. I have something to tell you that is very important, and I can't write it. It wouldn't be safe. Neither would it be safe for me to give you Jack's and my address. If Jack has given it to you and you have written it down anywhere, please destroy it. I'll come to see you at ten o'clock Wednesday evening. Please be alone so we can talk.

Until then I am,

Sincerely yours,
Sylvia Evers.

Sylvia Evers! The former Sylvia Sanderson, the dancer Jack had met down in South America. The girl for whom Jack had left Ronny and me. And as a result he had lost his job with The Sky High Oil Company. What could she want? I'd been wondering ever since the letter had arrived that morning. What did she have to tell me that Jack couldn't have told me that afternoon? Wednesday evening at ten. That was tonight!

Had she, perhaps, arrived earlier and killed Jack? Was she, perhaps, still in the house? I shivered and pulled a blanket up around Ronny's shoulders, although he wasn't the one who was cold.

When I heard the muted wail of a police siren, I said to Ronny, "You keep quiet now, and take another nap. I have to go downstairs." I leaned over and kissed his soft cheek and, leaving Boy in the room with him, went out and closed the door.

Quickly I ran down the stairs and hurried to open the front door before the hands of the law could ring the bell and bring Althea upstairs. I was just in time. Two husky policemen were running up the brownstone steps. The light from the hall chandelier struck their buttons and badges and made them look momentarily as if they were set with jewels. Boy, upstairs behind the closed door to Ronny's room, began to bark, and I called, "Keep still, Boy!" And he did.

The policemen looked me over carefully. "Having trouble here?" one of them asked.

I said, "Yes." They could see Jack's body lying there, halfway down the hall. I turned around to indicate it. Then I stared, and a cold chill ran all through me. The knife was gone from Jack's back!

I knew it couldn't have fallen out. It had been in too deep — almost up to the handle. And no one had been near the body to take it out. Or had they? Had the strange man I'd brought into the house taken it out? Or could Althea have come up from the kitchen and taken it? *That* I doubted. Then maybe it was some person about whom I knew nothing so far. Sylvia? I'd been upstairs with Ronny only for a few minutes.

The two policemen walked back to the body and knelt down beside it, examining it carefully. After a while one of them asked, "No weapon around?"

My visitor came from the sitting room and joined me. When he saw the knife was gone, he gave me a questioning look. "There was," he told the policeman. "There was a knife in his back, where the blood is, and the cut in his coat. The handle was sticking right out straight."

The two men looked up at him. "Who are you?" It was the other one who spoke this time.

My visitor rammed his hands into his trouser pockets. He was wearing a dark brown suit, beautifully fitted. I wondered if his hands were trembling. Mine were. He said, "I'm Dan Brewster. I'm a friend of Mrs. Evers. That is —" he nodded toward Jack's body — "the dead man used to be her husband. They were divorced. He came here this afternoon to see the little boy." He didn't look at me while he was speaking.

The policeman asked, "Did you kill him?"

"Certainly not!" Dan Brewster's answer

24

came quickly. Well, at least I knew his name now, but I couldn't help wondering how he knew the Evers name. Then it dawned on me. I'd mentioned it myself.

"Did you know him?" the policeman asked.

I thought the man named Dan Brewster hesitated for the fraction of a moment before he said, "No, I didn't know him."

The two men stood up and looked at him accusingly. The one who had asked the question demanded, "Can you prove you didn't kill him?"

He smiled slightly at that. "I hope so," he said.

With a quick move the policeman stepped over Jack's body and began searching my visitor, I supposed for a concealed weapon. I gave a sigh of relief when he found nothing. But he, the policeman, looked disappointed.

He turned to me and asked, "Who are you?"

I gulped. "I'm Mrs. Evers."

"Did you kill him?" he snapped.

I shook my head.

Outside, another siren screamed, louder than the first. The policeman who had just searched Dan Brewster said, "Pat, go tell the boys who have just come to watch the door. There's a basement door, too. Tell them to watch that. I'll phone the station and get the Homicide Squad started."

"Okay, Bill," Pat said, and went out.

The one called Bill asked, "Where's a phone?"

I led him through the dropped living room and up the two steps to the back sitting room, thinking this would give me a good chance to get Sylvia's letter. But it was gone! Unable to speak, due to the shock of this, I just pointed to the phone on the desk. As I did so, I noticed the green draperies at one of the windows were moving.

While Bill phoned, I walked quickly over to the window and pulled the draperies aside, expecting to find I knew not what.

There was nothing there. The window was open. It had been the wind moving the draperies. But I was sure the window had been closed. It had been too cold a day for open windows. I wondered if Dan Brewster had opened the window. I turned to him. He was standing in the doorway to the hall. "Did you open this?" I asked him.

He said, "No. And I'm sure it was closed when I was calling the police, because it was hot in here. But now it's cool."

Bill finished his call and turned to us. "Something bothering you?" he asked.

Dan Brewster pointed to the open window. "That wasn't open a few minutes ago, when I was in here phoning for you," he said.

The policeman stuck his head out of the window, and Dan Brewster went and looked over his shoulder. I didn't bother to look. I knew what they would see. Just outside was a narrow slanting roof that was the roof of the terrace outside the kitchen door. There was one just like it on the adjoining house on either side.

Behind each house was the usual New York back yard: a rectangular plot the width of the house and about eighteen or twenty feet deep. These plots are divided by board fences about seven feet high.

The houses on the other street had the same arrangement, and the yards of the two blocks were also divided by a board fence. This gave each yard semiprivacy, enclosing it on three sides by a board fence, and on the fourth side by its own house. Some of us painted our fences white, some brown and some green. Ours was green; a soft leafy green.

Most of the houses being privately owned in our particular neighborhood, each yard had been made into a small garden with a lawn and borders of flowers. Of course, this being February, everything was dead. But in the summer these small yards were pleasant and colorful.

I realized it would be an easy thing for a man to slide down the slanting roof and either get into one of the houses next door, or scale the fence and make a quick get-away in almost any direction.

There was a tree in the far left-hand corner of our yard, but I could see, over the heads of the two men, that the lights of the houses on the other street were shining. So if anyone was up in the tree, he could easily be seen, because the bare branches were few and far apart.

The policeman named Bill drew in his head, and Dan Brewster did, too. Bill closed and locked the window. "Who lives next door?" he asked me.

"On the left side, a doctor and his wife and two children. The other house is empty at present. Someone has recently bought it, and it is being remodeled."

He just grunted and went to inspect the other window, but it was closed and locked and there was no one lurking there. He unbuttoned his coat and took out a notebook and ball point pen. "Are you the one who phoned headquarters?" he asked Dan Brewster.

Dan said, "Yes."

"Name and address?"

"Daniel Brewster. At present I'm staying at The Eastview Hotel over on Madison Avenue."

"Business?"

He hesitated, glanced at me, then with tight lips said, "I'm with The Sky High Oil Company. I'm an engineer."

I gasped. That was the same company Jack worked for. Then perhaps this man *had* murdered Jack. If they worked for the same company, they must have known one another. I opened my mouth to speak, but the man gave me an almost imperceptible shake of his head and began showing the policeman his credentials.

The policeman examined them carefully and returned them. "My name is McCarthy," he said. "Bill McCarthy. You understand, everybody is a suspect until he is proved innocent."

Dan Brewster said, "I understand."

Bill McCarthy asked, "Who else is in the house?"

The logical thing would have been to ask me, but as long as I wasn't asked, I kept still and let Dan Brewster do the talking. He said, "Well, Mrs. Evers; and upstairs is her little boy. He's sick. A slight cold, I believe.

29

And there's a maid down in the kitchen. Her name is Althea. And as far as I know, there is no one else here. About half an hour ago, when the body fell out of that hall closet on top of me, there was a knife sticking out of its back. And now it's gone!"

"What kind of a knife?"

"Why, I don't remember. I think it had a black handle." He glanced at me for corroboration. I said, "I don't remember either."

The policeman didn't seem to be interested in what I thought. He continued questioning Dan Brewster. "And you couldn't tell what kind of a knife it was? A hunting knife or a kitchen knife?"

Dan Brewster said, "No, I couldn't tell. I don't know much about knives. In fact, I don't know anything about knives."

Suddenly there was a sharp knock on the front door. I started to go to answer it, but the policeman named Bill McCarthy came with me and shoved me aside. "I'll get it," he said. He flung the door open, and two men walked in. They were in plain clothes, but they came in with such an air of authority I guessed they were detectives. Bill said, "You got here quickly, Inspector. I haven't been over the house yet, or checked all the inmates." This made me angry. I didn't like being labeled an *inmate* in my own house. So I glared at him, but he didn't even notice.

The inspector nodded and walked down the hall to Jack's body. I turned and went upstairs. Nobody bothered to stop me, but I knew Dan Brewster saw me go. I didn't go into Ronny's room. His door was still closed, so I just stood in the second floor hall and listened to what was going on downstairs. I figured I had a right to know. If I leaned over the banister, I could see what was going on.

I saw the other detective, who had a large black suitcase, set it down in the hall out of the way of the front door. Then several more uniformed policemen came in. I'd been right about policemen swarming all over the place.

Bill told the inspector what he knew about the case and about Dan Brewster and me, which wasn't much. As he talked, he called the inspector by name. It was Joe Keen.

Another man came into the hall with a small black bag. Instinctively I knew he was the medical examiner. Joe Keen said, "Let me know how long he's been dead. As far as we know, it's a knife wound, but the weapon has disappeared."

The doctor knelt beside the body, and

Keen started to question Dan Brewster. "What do you know about this?" he demanded.

Dan said, "Well, I happened to be coming along the street about an hour or so ago when Mrs. Evers slipped on the ice. Her dog was after a cat. I caught her and saved her from a nasty fall. Then she discovered she'd hurt her ankle, so I helped her up the stoop."

"Then what?" Keen probed. He was treating Dan as if Dan were a schoolboy and he was the principal. I resented it, but what could I do? At least everything Dan had said was true.

"Well," Dan continued, "I started to light a cigarette and discovered I didn't have any matches, so I asked her if she had one. She said she didn't have one with her, but if I'd come in, there were some in the living room."

"And so you came in?" Keen asked.

Dan said, "Well, then she invited me to sit down. We talked a minute; then she offered me some sherry, because it was so cold out. But knowing her ankle was bad, I said I'd get it."

"Yes?" Keen urged.

"Well, she told me it was in the hall closet, so I came out into the hall. As I opened the door, the body fell out on me. It was standing in the closet, propped up by the closed door."

I shivered just hearing him tell it.

"How did the body get in the closet?" Keen demanded.

"How should I know?" Dan snapped. "As I figure it, he must have been getting himself a drink when he was stabbed in the back. He must have fallen over the counter of the bar and his murderer must have closed the door on him."

Keen let it go at that and spoke to the policemen grouped by the front door. "Better search the house, boys," he said.

Pat and a man they called Ed started to come up the stairs, and two others headed toward the back of the hall to go downstairs. I shrank back against the wall, and my heart began to pound. Then I heard Dan Brewster say, "Perhaps I'd better warn Mrs. Evers the police are on their way up."

"Why?" Keen asked. "To give her time to hide the weapon?"

I held my breath. What would Dan Brewster say to that? But I needn't have worried. He seemed able to cope with anything. Quietly he said, "We didn't have to phone the police until we were ready for them."

Keen grunted. He was a big man, easily

six feet and weighing about one hundred and sixty pounds. His face was rather red, and he had thin lips and small, piercing blue eyes. His brows were heavy and uneven and a darker brown than his sparse hair. I decided that even though he looked hardboiled, he was probably married and had children of his own.

Evidently Dan Brewster was figuring the same thing, because he had changed his tone of voice and was talking to him man to man. "Look, Inspector," he said, "we're in a spot here. At our feet is a dead man. Upstairs is his ex-wife, who I think has never stopped loving him, even though they were divorced. Also upstairs is the man's four-year-old son. Downstairs is the maid, who will probably get hysterical if she knows there's a dead body in the house." This almost made me smile, since I knew how practical and level-headed Althea was.

Keen said, "I'm almost in tears."

The policemen were waiting. So Dan tried again, bless him. He said, "Well, the child is sick. If suddenly two policemen burst into his room, it will frighten him."

Keen was silent a moment; then he said, "Hold it a minute, boys."

I let out my breath, which I hadn't realized I'd been holding. I decided it was time for me to help Dan out. I called, "Is that the police?"

Keen looked up the stairs, "That's right, lady," he said.

Ronny heard me and opened his door, and Boy rushed out of the room and began to growl and start down the stairs. I grabbed his collar. "Come back here!" I told him. "Be a good dog now." I dragged him back into Ronny's room and shut the door but let Ronny stay out in the hall. He asked in a shrill voice, "Mommy, who's downstairs?"

I said, "Ssshhh! There's been a little trouble. A leak or something. The police want to see that everything is all right."

"But, Mommy," Ronny shrilled, "police don't fix leaks. Plumbers do that."

I shook my head at him and put a warning finger over my lips. Looking down, I saw Keen scratch his head over his right ear. "We ought to get the kid out of here," he said.

Dan said, "Yes, we should," and started up the stairs, trying to push past the policemen who were waiting for further orders.

But Keen yelled at him, "Hey! Wait a minute! Where do you think you're going?"

Dan stopped. "I want to speak to Amelia — Mrs. Evers."

I could tell my first name had slipped out by mistake, and I wondered how he knew it. I was sure I hadn't mentioned it. The last name, yes, but not my first name. Then he must have known Jack at The Sky High Oil Company. And if so, he could easily have killed Jack there in the hall because of something that had happened down in South America. But if Jack had been alive when Dan Brewster went to the closet, he would have made a sound of some kind. And there hadn't been any sound but the dull thud the body had made as it fell.

Keen said, "Let's get her down here. Hey, Mrs. Evers, come down here!"

Dan Brewster looked up the stairs, and our eyes met. Something passed between us that made us allies, or conspirators, or whatever you want to call it. I said, "I don't like to leave my little boy. Won't you come up here, please?" Ronny was clinging to my skirt now, his blue eyes wide with excitement. More to himself than to me he said, "Real policemen!"

Keen started up the stairs, but Dan blocked his way. "Wait," he said. "We can't talk where the child will hear."

I hugged Ronny close to me. "I'd better take him to my mother's," I said, the idea suddenly occurring to me. "I'll get him

36

dressed right away. Will you get me a cab, Mr. Brewster?"

Dan said, "Get him dressed. We'll pick one up at the corner."

Keen said, "I'll see you later, Mrs. Evers." And he, Dan and the two policemen went down the stairs.

When Ronny and I came downstairs a few minutes later, I stayed close to the banister to shield Ronny so he could not see down into the hall, the men were all grouped by the front door. Dan obviously nervous now, took out a cigarette and lit it with a silver lighter. Keen raised his eyebrows. "And you came into the house for a match," he asked, "when you had a perfectly good lighter in your pocket?"

Dan's face flushed, and he glanced guiltily at me. "It doesn't always work," he said.

Keen reached for it and tried it several time. It worked each time. Without a word he handed it back to Dan.

I couldn't look at Dan after that, because it was now all too obvious he had gotten into my house under false pretenses. This, on top of the fact that he worked for the same company that Jack had, made it look suspicious. Thinking back on Jack's letters to me from South America, I couldn't remember his ever having mentioned a Dan Brewster.

37

"Well, I'd better get Ronny out of the house," I said. "Button your coat, dear. You don't want to catch more cold."

"But, Mommy," Ronny said, "you know I haven't a cold. That was just pretend, for Daddy."

I said, "Hush!"

Dan brought my hat and coat and helped me into the coat. I put the hat on my head as he opened the front door and told me, "Go straight out. I'll go out and get you a cab."

But Inspector Keen said, "Oh no, you won't. You'll stay here." Then he spoke to a policeman standing at the top of the stoop. "Manuel, take Mrs. Evers where she wants to go in one of the police cars. Then bring her back here."

Manuel, a nice-looking Puerto Rican with shiny black hair and liquid brown eyes, said, "Okay, boss."

Ronny looked up at me, his eyes wide and frightened now. "I don't want to go in the police car, Mommy," he wailed. "I wasn't a bad boy. I don't want to be arrested."

"You want to play with the siren?" Manuel asked him. "Make it go wheee, wheee, wheee?"

Ronny shook his head and gripped my hand, and I put an arm around him. "You aren't being arrested, darling," I told him.

"The nice policeman is just going to let us use his car as a taxi, to go to Grandma's."

"But I don't want to go to Grandma's!" Ronny wailed.

I said, "Ssshhh!" and pushed him out into the vestibule. Then suddenly I remembered Aunt Edna. How could I have forgotten her? I turned to Inspector Keen. "By the way, Inspector, when you search the house, please don't upset my aunt. Her room is on the top floor, and she's a bit — well, her mind is not — that is to say, she isn't well mentally."

Keen nodded. "I understand. To make a long story short, she's nuts."

I hesitated, then could only nod. Then my eyes met Dan's. I'd been able to feel him watching me. I asked, "Will you be here when I get back?"

He said, "Yes, I'll be here." I let Manuel take Ronny by the hand and me by the arm and help us down the now very slippery brownstone steps. I hated to admit it, even to myself, but I felt relieved to know Dan Brewster would be there when I returned. In spite of the circumstantial evidence against him, I couldn't believe him to be an evil person.

Chapter Three

I was only absent from the house about three quarters of an hour, and by the time I returned they had taken Jack's body away.

Dan Brewster was pacing up and down the length of the living room, in his hand a cigarette which he wasn't smoking. Inspector Keen was fussing around the hall closet. He looked at me when I came in. "I'm back," I said.

"So I see."

I hated to ask it, but I had to know. "Could the medical examiner tell when it happened?"

"About an hour before you found him."

I shuddered.

Dan came to the bottom of the two steps down to the dropped living room. "I was thinking," he said, "perhaps we'd better have a talk."

The clock on the dining room mantel struck eight. I'd completely forgotten about dinner. I asked Dan, "Have you had anything to eat?"

He said, "No. And I must admit I've been wondering about that dinner you said

Althea was preparing." I went down into the living room, took off my coat and hat and threw them down on the sofa. "Do you suppose the police would let us go downstairs?" I asked.

Inspector Keen heard me and called, "Sure. Go on down and eat. I have men posted at the front and in the back yard, so you're perfectly safe."

This surprised me, and I drew in a short, gasping breath. "You think there is danger? I mean that maybe there will be another — ?" I couldn't say the word.

Inspector Keen said, "You never can tell. Anyway, I'll have a couple of men on guard tonight."

I gave a little sigh and motioned Dan to follow me just as Bill McCarthy came down the stairs. Inspector Keen said to him, "Bill, take some of the boys and investigate the houses on either side of this one, as well as the ones that back up to this on the other street." Bill nodded and went out, and the inspector said, "By the way, Mrs. Evers, does your aunt always stay in her room?"

Dan and I were in the hall now, headed for the back stairs. I stopped, trying to avoid a chalk mark on the carpet which someone had put there to indicate where Jack's body had lain. I said, "Why, yes, nearly always, ex-

41

cept when Althea or I take her out for a walk."

"Yes."

"Shouldn't she be in a sanitarium?"

I hesitated before answering. "Why, yes, I think she should. But my mother doesn't agree with me. You see, she's my mother's sister."

"Then why doesn't your mother take care of her?"

"Because she only has a small apartment, and I have this big house." That seemed to be the end of the conversation, so I led Dan on through the hall and down to the basement floor, which was the usual kind to be found in every New York brownstone house. The narrow hall ran from the kitchen door, past the dining room door and on to the front where there was a door. Then came a small vestibule and an iron-grill gate that opened on an areaway three steps below the street level. I said, "You go on in the dining room, and I'll tell Althea we're here."

There was a light in the dining room, which was apple green and white, with the usual furniture and a small white marble fireplace. Two windows looked out on the areaway, and a door at the other end of the room opened into a butler's pantry, which in turn led to the kitchen.

When Althea saw me, she just stared for a moment, her black face practically white with fear and horror, and I realized I should have been the one to tell her about our tragedy, not have left it for the police to do. But I had been so upset and shocked I hadn't thought.

Her fat body was shaking beneath her neat black dress with its white collar and cuffs, and she tucked her fat hands beneath the small tailored white apron so I wouldn't see how they were trembling. She was fifty years old, and her hair was partially gray. I said, "I'm sorry to have held up dinner so long, Althea. But we're ready now. And I have a guest."

She stared at me. She was crying now, tears running down her face. "Oh, my poor Mister Evers," she moaned. She sniffled. "And *you*, my poor lamb, I didn't think you'd do it! I didn't think you *would!* You said, 'If he ever does anything to hurt Ronny, I'll kill him.' But I didn't think you would! You're so kind, and you loved him so."

She had a nice speaking voice and a dignified manner, but I realized she was excited and didn't know what she was saying. So I said sharply, "Althea, keep still!" Surely Dan Brewster must have heard her in the dining room, if not Inspector Keen upstairs in the hall. To tell the truth, I was surprised at her reaction, because she had always been so sensible but of course we'd never had anything like this happen before.

I went to her and put a comforting arm around her shaking shoulders. "Come now," I said gently, "and pull yourself together. I'm going to need you to take care of me until this thing is straightened out." I knew this was a sure way to appeal to her, for whenever any of us needed taking care of, we could always count on Althea to do it. Then I asked, "Did you say this to any of the policemen?"

She bowed her head, and the tears ran down her cheeks. "Yes, I'm afraid I did. I was so shocked. I went upstairs to take your aunt her dinner tray — and there he was." She took her hands from beneath her apron and put them over her face.

"What did he or they say? I mean the policemen."

"It was that one named Keen. He asked me how long I'd been in this family. And I told him the truth — six years, ever since you married Mr. Evers. And before that I worked for your mother."

I said, "Well, that was all right. Anything else?"

44

"Yes. He asked me if you and Mr. Evers ever quarreled."

"And what did you say?"

"I said, 'No, sir. They never quarreled.' And he said, 'They just lived together, not getting along very well, but not quarreling?' " She took her hands away from her face, got a paper towel and wiped her eyes. "And I told him, 'No, sir. They got along fine. They were in love. They were crazy about each other.' "

I patted her arm. "Good for you," I said.

"But that man, he kept on asking questions. He said, 'But then why would Mrs. Evers want to kill her husband?' So I just talked right back to him. I said, 'She didn't want to. She loved him.' Then he tried to trick me. He said, 'But you said — ?' And I said, 'No, sir. I didn't say anything. I was excited. I got upset for a minute when I saw him.' "

"Then what?" I asked.

"Well, then he told me to go on upstairs with the tray with your aunt's dinner. So I did. I went through the sitting room so I wouldn't have to — Then when I came downstairs, that man — that strange man — he and I got fingerprinted." She looked at me accusingly. "*Who is* that strange man?" she demanded.

"A friend of mine. His name is Mr. Dan Brewster."

"I never saw him before. How do we know he didn't do it?"

"I'm sure he didn't. He was out with me when it happened. And he's very hungry. May we have some dinner now?"

Althea wiped her face with the paper towel. "I suppose so," she said, and I left her and went into the dining room. My ankle was aching, and I couldn't keep from limping a little.

Dan was waiting and held my chair for me, then sat down opposite me. I said, "Our dinner will be very simple. But if you're hungry, maybe you won't mind."

He smiled at me. "Anything at all will do." Then he asked, "Hadn't you better do something about that ankle?"

I shrugged. "Oh, it isn't bad," I fibbed. "Althea will bind it for me later." Then I said, "I'm sorry you got involved in this."

He met my eyes across the table. "I owe you an explanation," he said. "It's my own fault I'm involved in it."

I guess I gave a start, because he said, "I didn't do it, if that's what you're thinking."

I toyed with my fork and lowered my eyes. "I'm sure you didn't."

Althea brought us food. Her hands trembled as she served it. I asked, "Althea, was anybody here this afternoon except Mr. Evers?"

She gave Dan a baleful look. "Nobody but *him!* And then all those policemen."

Dan and I began to eat. It was hamburger with onions, string beans and baked potato. It was ambrosia. I was starved. But it stuck in my throat. "Are you sure?" I asked. "No workmen or delivery boys? Not a soul?"

Althea thought a moment. "No, ma'am. No one but the grocery boy." It was quite apparent she didn't approve of my visitor, and she returned to her kitchen, accompanied by her righteous indignation.

For several moments Dan and I resumed eating in silence. Then I broke the silence by saying, "You wanted to talk to me?"

He said, "Yes. You probably noticed I called you Amelia upstairs in the hall. And a few minutes ago I spoke of your husband as Jack."

I was just picking at my food. I said, "Yes, I did notice."

He laid down his knife and fork and gave me his undivided attention. "Well," he said, "you heard me tell the policeman I work for The Sky High Oil Company."

I nodded.

Looking me right in the eyes, he told me,

"I was down in Venezuela with Jack."

I dropped my fork and met his eyes accusingly. "Then you *did* do it."

"I did not!" He had a square jaw, and it tightened. "For a while Jack and I were very close. Stuck out in the wilds down there, there wasn't much to do with our free time but talk. Jack talked a lot about you and Ronny. He used to read me your letters. And he used to read me those he wrote you."

I felt my face getting warm. "Oh, I'm surprised he would do that," I said, remembering some of our more intimate letters. There was the one where I'd written:

. . . At night I look over at the empty bed and feel as if I were all alone on a great big desert without a living soul within miles. But of course that is silly, because I am surrounded by people. I have Ronny in the next room in his junior bed with the little flight of stairs. And then of course there is Althea up in her room on the top floor, and Aunt Edna. And if I ever want to go anywhere that necessitates an escort, I can always call on Bryan.

But getting back to Ronny — I think maybe I'll bring him in with me, maybe even put him in your bed, so when I look over there I'll see him and feel you are close. For

Ronny is partly you, dear, and partly me.
But mostly you —

Then there was Jack's letter to me in which he had said:

I wish you could have come down here with me, but I realize you couldn't leave Aunt Edna. I'm glad she has been a little better lately. However, I still think your mother ought to let you put her in a sanitarium.
And don't have too much to do with that Bryan. I don't like him. You know that.

Then there was the letter he wrote me after he'd met Sylvia Sanderson. He wrote:

A few days ago several of us got away for a while and went to Caracas. It was the first time in months we'd been away from this God-forsaken place, and boy, did women look good to us — especially an American girl who was dancing in a night club. Her name is Sylvia Sanderson, and she has the most gorgeous blonde hair I've ever seen. Or maybe it's just because I haven't seen any blonde hair in so long. Yours is red, isn't it, darling? I've almost forgotten. Eighteen months can seem very long, almost like eigh-

teen years. Maybe you should have come along with me. Then we could have had one of those little houses in the company village, and I could have gotten to see you once in a while. That way, I wouldn't be so interested in blondes. As it is, being one of the so-called single men, I'm stuck in the farthest outpost, where there's nothing but men and oil wells.

I wonder what it will be like to see you again. Will everything drop into place and make the old familiar pattern, or will we be strangers?

The one I will never forget was the one he wrote me asking for a divorce. I was so shocked! That was the time I'd said to Althea, "If he ever does anything to hurt Ronny, I'll kill him!"

He wrote:

Dear Amelia:

This will probably be a shock to you, but I want a divorce. I want to marry Sylvia Sanderson. I know it's a dirty trick to play on you, but men aren't angels, and there are some things too strong for them to fight. This is it for me. I'm crazy about the dizzy blonde, and I know you wouldn't want me back, knowing that. She is getting a divorce from her husband so she can marry me.

There was more in it, but I couldn't bear to think of it. Tears came to my eyes as I remembered.

Dan said, "I'm sorry, but you see, Jack was lonely and had to talk to someone. And as time went on, even though it wasn't any of my business, I couldn't help feeling Jack made a mistake to get himself mixed up with that girl. But lots of men get their values mixed when they're stuck in some lonely spot for too long. If this hadn't happened today, I'm pretty sure Jack would have realized his mistake and come back to you and Ronny eventually."

I had to cover my face with my hands so he wouldn't see me cry. I guess I embarrassed him, because he sat quietly, not saying a word. After a few minutes Althea came in with a pitcher of ice water. When she saw me crying, she thumped the pitcher down on the table and put an arm around my shaking shoulders. "There, there, honey," she said. "Eat your dinner now. You're going to need your strength."

I took my hands away from my face, and across the table Dan handed me a clean handkerchief. As I used it, Althea began to refill our water glasses. "I've been thinking," she said. "That grocery boy isn't really a *boy*. He's a *man*. He's Hungarian or Romanian or something like that."

"His nationality doesn't have anything to do with it," Dan said quietly. "But I don't see how he could have done it — or why."

"I don't either." I agreed. "He just comes in with the groceries and then goes right out again. And he didn't even know Mr. Evers."

Dan asked Althea, "Did you see him go out the street door?"

She stood with the pitcher in mid-air. "No, sir. He put the groceries on the kitchen table, then went out. There was a lot of them, and he had to make two trips. Then I heard him walk down the hall and close the door. But I didn't actually see him go out with my own eyes."

"Did you hear the gate close?" Dan asked.

Althea shook her head. "I couldn't say. I had the radio going in the kitchen. I guess he closed the gate all right. He always does."

Dan asked her, "What is the name of the grocer?"

I answered for her. "The Madison Food Market. It's one of the few privately owned food stores in the neighborhood. I don't like supermarkets. So I always use the smaller places."

"Would it be open this time of night?"

I shook my head. "No. They close at six. Besides, I'm sure Nikki is all right. He's been with the store for about six months and is in and out of the house every day. There wouldn't be any reason for him to —"

Dan began eating again. "You're probably right," he said. "But everybody should be checked."

Althea heaved a big sigh and began gathering up the soiled dishes; then she shuffled out to the kitchen with the main course dishes and brought us dessert: a creamy rice pudding, small iced cup cakes and coffee. When she'd returned to the kitchen, I said, "Please try not to upset Althea. She's not only my maid, but my very dear friend."

Dan's face flushed, and I managed a smile for him. "And now, would you mind telling me why you are here? I mean, how you happened to be walking along this block when I slipped on the ice?"

He drew in a long breath and looked directly into my eyes. "I've had you on my mind," he said, "ever since those letters. You see, Jack also showed me color snapshots of you and Ronny. I know it sounds silly, but there was something about you — that lovely dark red hair, your gray-green eyes, your smile —"

"You can't expect me to believe that."

"I can't expect anybody to believe anything," he said rather hopelessly. "But what I'm telling you is true. After Jack left the oil fields to meet that girl in Caracas, the situation worried me. You didn't look like the kind of a girl who deserved a deal like the one you got. And I began to wish I knew you, so I could — well, do something for you."

I smiled, ruefully, I guess. "As for instance?" I asked.

He looked at me thoughtfully for a moment. "I don't know exactly," he admitted. "I just had an uncontrollable urge to see you and to know you. I had a vacation due me, so I made up my mind I'd use it to come to New York and see you. But I couldn't get up enough nerve to come in and introduce myself. So I walked up and down this block for quite a while this afternoon, wondering what I could say to you if I rang the bell and presented myself." He smiled ruefully. "I couldn't say 'How do you do, Mrs. Evers. I'm Dan Brewster. And as you see, I am tall, dark, and some women think I'm handsome; why, I've never been able to figure out.' Nor could I go on to say, 'I'm thirty-three years old, unmarried, and I'm head over heels in —' Well, we'll forget that part of it. And least of all could I say, 'I work for

The Sky High Oil Company, and I knew your husband down in Venezuela. That's how I heard about you, because when Jack was still a nice guy, and we were out in that God-forsaken hole with nothing in sight but a few shacks and acres of oil wells, he used to show me pictures of you and read me your letters to him and his letters to you. And if you'll pardon me, I think you got a dirty deal and he's a louse. Therefore I am no longer his friend, but I would like very much to be yours.' If I'd said all that, you'd have thrown me out on my ear."

I couldn't help laughing. That was what he had been trying to make me do, so I'd relax a little. I said, "Maybe I wouldn't have. But anyway, fate took a hand, and you got a break when Boy obligingly chased the cat and I slipped on the ice."

He smiled with one side of his mouth, and the look in his eyes made me feel all nice and warm inside. "That's about it," he said.

"You're sure you didn't release the cat at the psychological moment?"

He grinned. "Give you my word." He began to eat his dessert and drink his coffee. "You know," he told me, "a lot of people believe in fate. As they used to say a couple of generations ago, 'If you were born to be hanged, you'll never drown.' "

"And do you believe that?"

"To a certain extent. In some ways I'm more or less of a fatalist."

"Then you believe that was Jack's fate?"

"Perhaps. But I wasn't thinking that just then. I was thinking perhaps it was fate that I should have been here to save you from the shock of discovering him, and to help you through whatever may be ahead."

Tears suddenly filled my eyes. "You sound very kind and thoughtful. Perhaps I shall be glad I slipped on the ice."

"Perhaps," he said.

We ate in silence for a few moments; then he said, "Your Althea is a good cook."

I said, "Yes, she is."

"I'll bet you are a good cook yourself."

I shrugged. "Yes, I can cook. But it was Althea who taught me. My mother fed us out of cans, when we weren't on the road with a play she and Dad were in. Then we ate in restaurants."

"Oh, you're an actress?" He seemed surprised.

"No," I told him. "But my folks were, and Althea was my mother's personal maid for a long time. She practically brought me up, even though she was married."

"Did she and her family live with you?"

"No. They had an apartment up in

Harlem. Her husband was a song and dance man. He worked in night clubs in Harlem. But that was about all he could get. When Althea was young, she was on the stage herself for a while."

"I noticed she spoke very nicely."

"Yes, she does. But back in her day, there wasn't much chance for colored people in the theater. Oh, she had a few parts as a maid, but that didn't get her far, and there was nowhere else to go, so she had to give up. Then she was a wardrobe woman for a while, just so she could be around the theater. She loved it. Then her husband died of pneumonia, so my mother took her as her personal maid and she came to live with us. And she always traveled with us."

He asked, "Didn't you ever want to act?"

"No. I was the maverick of the family. I didn't seem to have any talent — in anything. So I married before I finished college."

"Did you meet Jack in college?"

"No. We had mutual friends."

"How old are you, if that isn't an impertinent question?"

"Twenty-four."

"You must have been glad to get a home of your own."

"I was. And I loved being married." I

57

guess I blushed a little as I said that, so I hurried on. "I mean, when Jack and I were first married, and up until the time he went down to South America, we were very happy." Then I said a stupid thing. I said, "You say you're not married?"

He replied, "No. To tell the truth, I haven't known many girls in my life. Dad was an engineer, like myself, and we always lived in some out-of-the-way place. My mother died when I was eight, and Dad kept me with him until I was twelve. Then I went to a boys' boarding school. And in college I had to study too hard. You see, I'm not one of those bright boys who picks things up quickly. I have to work like the devil on everything."

I had to smile at that, because he seemed very intelligent and smart. "You're probably just being modest," I told him.

The inspector came downstairs, and I asked him, "Will you have some coffee?"

He sat down at the table. "Don't mind if I do," he said. "As a matter of fact, I want to talk to you two some more. And incidentally, my name is Joe Keen."

"If there's anything we can do to help, Inspector Keen," I said, "I'm sure both myself and Mr. Brewster will be glad to cooperate." I pressed my foot on a bell installed beneath the table, and Althea appeared at the door. I said, "Coffee for Inspector Keen, please, Althea."

She said, "Yes, ma'am," and disappeared.

The inspector looked Dan over carefully. "We've checked on you, Brewster," he said. "You're everything you claimed to be."

Dan said, "Thank you," miraculously keeping sarcasm out of his voice.

Inspector Keen said, "Now, tell me just why you happened to be in this neighborhood at the time of the murder."

Dan looked at me, and I said, "Tell him what you've just told me." So he did.

"Sounds logical," Keen conceded when Dan finished. "We'll check on it more thoroughly tomorrow."

Althea brought the inspector's coffee, gave him a dirty look and returned to the kitchen.

Keen said, "My men have investigated every house all around the block. There didn't seem to be any clues, and no one saw or heard anything unusual. The house next door that way —" he jerked his head to indicate the direction — "is empty and evidently being redecorated. There was no one there. The doctor and his family on the other side didn't hear or see anything, nor did the people in that apartment building at the end of the block."

"But how could Jack have been killed, right in his own house?" I asked, a chill slithering up my back at the thought.

Inspector Keen gave me a sharp glance. "I thought you were divorced?" he snapped.

My face began to feel warm, and I knew I was blushing. "We were."

"Then *was* the house his *own* house?"

I muddled my spoon around in what was left of my rice pudding. "Well, no," I said. "He deeded it to me when we were getting the divorce. You see, he had a substantial private income from his family, in addition to his salary from the oil company."

"What about his family?" Keen asked.

I hated all this prying into our personal affairs, but I realized it was just routine under the circumstances. I said, "He was an only child. His father died when he was very young. He lived with his mother until we were married, and she died soon afterward, leaving him very well off."

"Did your husband leave a will?" Keen asked between sips of coffee.

"I don't know. I suppose he did." I was quite surprised at the question.

"Did he marry again?"

A sigh escaped me before I said, "Yes, he did."

"Did you know the woman?"

"No." This was getting to be too much for me, and I began to feel faint. I gulped some coffee.

"Ever see her?" Keen persisted.

"No."

He turned his attention from me to Dan, pointed at him with his spoon and said, "If you and this man Evers were so chummy down in South America, you ought to know something about this."

Dan looked unhappy. "A man's confidences are sacred," he said quietly.

"Not in a case of murder!"

Feeling sorry for Dan's predicament, I said, "It's all right to tell him what you know."

"Come on; hurry up," Keen growled, drinking his coffee noisily now. So Dan began to tell his story of how Jack had confided in him and shown him pictures of Ronny and me, and how he had become interested in us even before he'd seen us. As he talked, beads of perspiration came out on his forehead. When he finished, Keen said, "That gives you a very good motive for murdering your husband, Mrs. Evers."

Again faintness swept over me, and I rested my head on a hand, the elbow propped on the table. "Yes, doesn't it?" I said, meeting Keen's accusing eyes. "Only I didn't."

He clattered his coffee cup down on its saucer. "How do we know you didn't!"

I was able to hold up my head now without the support of my hand. Getting angry always gives me strength. I said, with what I hoped was dignity, "Well, to begin with, I was out."

"I know that. You went out about three, and you came back about five — with Brewster here."

I nodded.

"But you could have killed your husband before you went out."

"Except that you told me your medical examiner said he had only been dead about an hour."

Keen said, "Um. So if you were out for two hours, what were you doing during that time? You couldn't have walked the streets with the dog all that time."

"No, I didn't," I admitted. "I took the dog to have his nails clipped. The vet said we'd have to wait quite a while. So I left the dog and went to the beauty parlor to have my hair done."

"Give me the name and address of the vet and the beauty parlor," he demanded, taking out a notebook and pen.

I gave him the information, adding, "In other words, you don't believe me?"

I guess Dan could see I was getting angrier and angrier, because he interrupted and began to tell Keen about the grocery boy. But Keen didn't seem interested. He said, "Okay. We'll check on him in the morning." Then he said, "You can go to your hotel now, Brewster. But don't try to do a disappearing act, because you're still a suspect."

I got up from the table and surprised myself, as well as the men, by asking, "Couldn't Mr. Brewster stay here for the night? We have plenty of room."

Keen stood up and looked at me with raised brows. "Why, I suppose so," he said, "if you want him to. But there's always the chance that maybe *he* killed your husband."

"Oh, don't be ridiculous!" I cried impatiently.

Dan, looking as surprised as Keen did, met my eyes, and the thought flashed through my mind that maybe *he* had taken Sylvia's letter from the desk in the sitting room. If he had, he would be doubly surprised at my suggestion. Finally he said, "That is very kind of you, and very brave, because I really *am* still a suspect."

"So am I," I reminded him. "Are you

afraid to stay in the house with me?"

This caused him to look embarrassed, and he said, "I would like very much to be allowed to spend the night in the house, in case you should need me. But I'd better go down to my hotel and get some toilet articles and pajamas and things. I should be back soon after ten."

Was he trying to tell me he knew about Sylvia's letter?

Keen said, "Manuel will run you down and back."

We all started for the stairs, I first, Dan next. Keen left us, went out into the areaway and said something to the policemen grouped in front of the house, then came in and followed us up to the first floor.

The entire floor was empty of police now. Dan went down into the dropped living room to pick up his hat and coat, and I was right beside him. But when he reached for his hat, he stopped, and a strange expression came over his face. Then I saw what he was looking at. Speared to the crown of his hat with a knife was a small piece of paper. On it was printed:

YOU KEEP OUT OF THIS

Chapter Four

Inspector Keen came down into the room and saw what we were staring at. "Don't touch it!" he commanded. He took his handkerchief and carefully removed the knife from the hat, leaving a clean slit in the top of it. "Too bad," he said. "Looks like a new hat."

Dan said, "It is. But a hat is unimportant. I shudder to think what that knife would feel like in my back."

Keen was examining the knife. "Looks like a knife anybody would have in his kitchen — a carving knife or a bread knife." He looked at Dan. "Was this the kind you saw in the back of the corpse?"

At Keen's brutal words, my knees gave way. I got to a chair and collapsed.

Dan nodded an affirmative answer to Keen's question. "It might almost be the same knife," he told him.

The inspector wrapped the handkerchief around it. His back was toward the sitting room, and I decided it was a good chance to go and see if I could find Sylvia's letter. I got up, my legs still feeling hollow, and hurried toward the back room. I moved quietly, and either Keen didn't hear me or he pretended he didn't. But Dan saw me and quickly began talking about knives, about which he had already said he knew nothing. I had the feeling he was trying to cover for me; to give me a chance to do whatever it was I wanted to do.

Going up the two steps into the sitting room, I searched frantically around the desk for Sylvia's letter. Finally I had to give up and return to the living room. Desperately I wished I knew who had it. Could the one who had murdered Jack and then escaped out the window in the sitting room have taken it? Could it have blown out the open window for one of the neighbors to find? My heart sank.

As I joined the two men down in the living room, Dan said to Keen, "I guess I'll go along now. Will you be here when I get back?"

Keen said, "No. I guess I've done all I can tonight. I'll have the boys go over the house again, just to be on the safe side." He sighed and looked at the handkerchief-wrapped knife in his hand. "I don't see how the devil this knife got into your hat," he said. "We searched the house thoroughly before. The boys are out front, and there is a man in the back yard, so no one could have gotten into the house again without being seen." He scratched the back of his neck thoughtfully.

Dan asked, "How about the roof?"

Keen snapped the fingers of the hand he'd just scratched his neck with. "Holy Christmas!" he cried. "And I'm supposed to be a detective!" He dashed to the front door and called, "Manny!" The handsome Puerto Rican policeman came in. "Yes, boss," he said.

Keen said, "Come on. The house has a roof. Why in blazes didn't you fellows think of that?"

Manuel winked at Dan and me. "I didn't realize we were supposed to think, boss."

Keen cursed under his breath and started up the stairs, and Manuel followed him.

As soon as they were out of sight, Dan said, "Come over here." He walked to the bookcase at the left side of the two steps up to the sitting room, took from a shelf above his head a book of poetry, opened it and took out Sylvia's letter. Giving it to me, he said, "I found this under the desk when I went to phone."

I grabbed it. It was out of the envelope. I'd thrown the envelope into the wastebasket when I'd opened the letter that morning. "I suppose you've read it?" I said, glancing up at him.

"Yes. I'm going out now to try to head her off. I just gave my pajamas and things as an excuse."

I stared at him, incredulous. "But I *want* to see her!" I told him. "She may know something. And I'd like to see what she looks like." I went up into the sitting room, put the letter and the book on the desk and idly picked up a bronze paper knife. It was long, slender and very sharp at the point. The thought flashed through my mind that it would be an excellent murder weapon. Then, frightened at the thought, I tossed the paper knife back onto the desk as if it had burned my fingers.

Dan stood watching me for a moment. I thought he looked apprehensive. Had my thoughts showed? He said, "And you would like to be the one to tell her about Jack?" The look in his eyes made me shiver, and I had the feeling that maybe he didn't like me as much as he'd pretended to. I chewed at my upper lip. "In a way, yes," I admitted. I met his questioning eyes, and I knew mine must have been cold, because I felt cold inside and out. Gritting my teeth, I said, "I want that woman to be allowed to come in here!"

In response to the determination I was showing, Dan said, "And I am going to make sure she doesn't." He turned from me and hurried down the two steps to the living room, across it, grabbed his coat and cut hat, went up the two steps to the hall and opened the front door. But he was too late to accomplish his mission. I heard him say, "Oh, hello, Sylvia."

I quickly followed him and joined him at the door. The girl standing there stared at me and I at her. I tried to feel hate toward her, but strangely enough, suddenly I felt nothing — nothing at all.

She was a tall, slender girl with heavy blonde hair which she quite evidently helped to glisten like burnished gold. She had it piled on top of her head like a crown, and I had to admit she looked stunning. Her coat was a mini-leopard, and under it she had a green suit with a white blouse. The suit skirt was short, showing several inches of shapely legs above her knees. She had on high black boots with heels. There was a green purse under her arm, and there were gold hoop earrings fastened to her small, well shaped ears. A policeman was holding her arm. She said, "This policeman won't let me in. Are you Mrs. Evers? If you are, I have an appointment with you." Then she asked Dan, "What's the matter here? Why are the policemen all around?"

"Do you know this girl?" the policeman asked Dan. He couldn't see me from where he was standing.

Dan said, "Yes, of course. I met her down in South America."

Sylvia looked surprised, so Dan mentioned the name of the night club in Caracas, adding, "I was the fellow who used to come there with Jack."

Sylvia drew in her breath. "Oh," she said. "Oh yes, I remember you now."

I had to admit Sylvia was pretty, in a cheap theatrical way. But I couldn't see how Jack could have fallen for her hard enough to give up me, Ronny and his home. I said, "Won't you come in, Sylvia? I'm Mrs. Evers. Mr. Brewster was just leaving. Come in. We can have a nice quiet little talk — alone." To the policeman I said, "It's all right, Officer. This lady is a friend of mine."

Sylvia came in, and I smiled at the policeman and closed the door. I led Sylvia to the fireplace, and she seemed grateful for the warmth. She sank down in the cherry brocade chair where Jack used to sit. "I have to talk to you," she said.

I sat opposite her on the sofa. "All right. Go ahead."

"Jack's going to leave me," she said, her face looking pale and, I thought, tired.

I said, "Oh? Why?" Which was a stupid question.

"I think it's another woman." She took a cigarette from a pack in her purse, scrambled for matches, found them, lit the cigarette and began to smoke nervously.

"What makes you think that?" I asked her.

She looked over at me, and her eyes, which for the first time I saw were a dark brown, looked frightened. "He doesn't pay much attention to me any more. I've been wondering if maybe he was coming back to you?"

Maybe it was silly of me, but I actually felt sorry for her. "No. *That* I am sure of," I told her.

She gave a sigh that could have been one of relief. "If he leaves me now, I think I'll kill him!" she said vehemently.

"That won't be necessary," I told her, "because he was murdered here this afternoon. Didn't you know?"

She stared at me, her brown eyes seeming to enlarge and pop out from their sockets. "Oh, my God!" she cried. "*No!* Who did it?"

"I thought you might know."

She stared at me. "No! No! How should I know?"

"You just said you'd kill him if he left you."

71

She stared at me. She looked scared. "No! I didn't mean it. Honest I didn't!" She began to cry and threw her cigarette butt into the fire. "Oh dear!" she wailed. "What am I going to do now? I'm going to have a baby, and I haven't got any money."

"I'll give you some," I told her. After all, she *was* in a spot. My checkbook was in the desk in the sitting room. I got up to get it, and she followed me. "Surely you must have *some* money," I said as I took the book from the drawer.

"No, honest, I haven't. Jack never gave me any cash. He gave me charge accounts everywhere, but not cash. Did he treat *you* that way?"

I said, "Well, no." Then I asked, "Was that all you wanted to see me about?"

She was standing at the end of the desk, facing the door into the hall. She said, "No. I wanted to warn you about —"

I wrote her a check for a hundred dollars and handed it to her. I said, "I have some cash upstairs. Wait here, and I'll go up and get it." I looked up at her, thinking she'd at least say, "Thank you," but she didn't. She just stared ahead of her, over my head, and didn't even take the check. So I laid it on the desk and went down through the living room and into the front hall and up the stairs to my bedroom, where I had some cash in a small safe.

I guess I was upstairs about ten minutes. When I got back downstairs, Sylvia was lying in the middle of the floor in the sitting room, on her back, and the bronze paper knife was in her heart. Her fur coat and suit coat were open, and blood was oozing out around the knife onto her white blouse. Beside her, on the floor, was her green purse. The check I'd written for her was still on the desk, together with the letter she'd written me and the book of poetry Dan had hidden it in.

I knelt down beside her to see if I could detect any breathing, the five twenty-dollar bills I'd brought from upstairs still clutched in my hand.

She wasn't breathing. I managed to get to my feet, and for several moments I was too shocked to move. Then I screamed, and seemingly from nowhere, policemen began to arrive — from downstairs, from outside. I tried to tell them what I knew, but my voice wouldn't make any sound. All I could do was point to the dead girl at my feet. Manuel came to me and helped me into the desk chair. I nodded a thank-you. Policemen kept coming in from outside and kept asking me questions, but I couldn't answer.

They picked up the check and asked me about it. I pointed to the dead girl. "It was for her?" a policeman named Donovan asked.

I nodded. I was still clutching the five twenty-dollar bills. He flicked them with his hand. "These for her, too?" he asked. He had a gun in his hand.

I nodded.

"That why you killed her?" he demanded. "Because she was blackmailing you?"

I shook my head. Just then the front door opened, and Dan Brewster came in. He'd certainly made a quick trip. When he saw the policeman standing over me with a gun in his hand, he dropped his bag on the floor and came down the two steps into the living room in one stride, ran through the living room and came up the two steps to the sitting room in one leap. "What happened?" he asked.

Then he saw Sylvia, and I saw fright come into his eyes. Donovan said, "I heard a scream, and I rushed in and —" He took a better grip on his gun, then added succinctly, "At least *this* is *one* murder there won't be any argument about."

Dan looked at me questioningly, and somehow I managed to get my voice to work. "I went upstairs to get her some cash," I told him. "I was only gone a few minutes. When I came back, she was like that."

"Did you hear her scream?" Dan asked me.

I shook my head. "No. I didn't. I don't think she did. It was I who screamed — when I saw her. I didn't even touch her. I just was looking at her —" I nodded toward Donovan. "That's when he found me."

The next hour or so was a repetition of the afternoon-medical examinations, flash bulbs as photographers took pictures; questions and more questions. I had to tell them that Sylvia was my divorced husband's new wife, and they were a bit skeptical about that, because it seems that the credentials in Jack's pockets didn't mention her name; only mine and my address.

They questioned Althea, and she said she hadn't heard anything. She and the policemen in the kitchen had been listening to a small radio. She gasped when she saw Sylvia, but she didn't say anything. She very carefully avoided meeting my eyes.

Donovan had been the only one on watch out front. He admitted he'd felt cold and had stood in the vestibule for a few minutes to get out of the wind. I don't know where Manuel came from. I thought he'd driven

Dan to his hotel, but he hadn't. Dan had taken a taxi. Later, I learned that Manuel had been down in the basement. When Inspector Keen, who had arrived by that time, heard Donovan's excuse for not being where he should have been, he gave him a dirty look. "Then anyone could have gone in through the basement, and you wouldn't have seen him?" he asked.

Donovan looked guilty. "I thought it would be all right," he said. "Hugh and Manny were down in the kitchen."

Keen made a disparaging sound in his throat and told me, "I'm afraid I'll have to get your aunt's fingerprints this time."

"Oh, but surely you can't suspect her?" I cried, really frightened now.

Keen shrugged. "No, I don't," he said. "I suspect *you*. But I'm going to get her prints just the same."

"What about the roof?" Dan asked, as he had earlier in the evening.

This time Keen glared at him. "I hooked the skylight the last time we looked there," he snapped. "Besides, if anyone had come in that way, the old lady would have seen him and yelled."

I wasn't too sure about that, but I didn't say anything. As it happened, Aunt Edna was sitting quietly listening to her radio when he and I went upstairs, and he was able to get her fingerprints without upsetting her too much. I kept talking soothingly to her and told her I was going to have her come down and sleep in my room with me. She seemed pleased at the idea, and I got her night things and took her downstairs as soon as the inspector left us. At the head of the stairs, he stopped and told me, "Come downstairs as soon as you get her settled."

I said, "All right," and did as he'd asked.

As soon as he saw me, he said, "I'm sorry, Mrs. Evers, but you'll have to come over to headquarters this time."

I sighed. "All right."

Dan said, "Wait a minute, Amelia. Haven't you a lawyer?"

This surprised me. "Why, yes," I said.

"Call him."

I looked questioningly at Inspector Keen. "That's your privilege," he told me. "Tell him to meet us at headquarters."

I went to the phone and dialed Bryan's number. When I got him, I said, "Bryan, this is Amelia. Something terrible has happened." As I was talking to him, I couldn't help remembering Jack's letter telling me, "Don't see too much of that guy. I don't like him."

Into the phone Bryan asked, "What?

Something happened to you?"

I said, "No. That is, not exactly. Not yet."

"Then what is it? Are you in trouble?"

"Yes, yes, I am, Bryan. Can you meet me at the police station right away? The nearest one to here — wherever it is."

"Police station?" Bryan yelled. "Darling, what's wrong? Have you been in a traffic accident?"

"No!" I cried, getting impatient. Bryan meant well, but he was very trying sometimes. "Oh please!" I said. "I can't explain now. Just come. Quickly, please!" I was dangerously near tears, and my voice was trembling. "I need you, Bryan!" I almost sobbed.

"All right, darling," he said, and I could tell he was excited. "Whatever it is, don't worry. I'll take care of everything for you."

When we reached the police station, he was just getting out of his car, and I'd never been so glad to see him. He was tall, slender, but with an athletic build. His hair was prematurely gray, which gave him a distinguished look. When he saw me getting out of the police car, he rushed over to me, and I held out my hands to him.

"What is it?" he asked anxiously. "What's happened?" He took my hands in his and looked down at me with a worried look in his light blue eyes. I knew he was in love

78

with me, but I never could forget that Jack had not liked him.

"Oh, Bryan!" I cried, and before I knew it I was crying on his shoulder. Subconsciously I realized I wasn't being fair to him, because I didn't return his love, but at the moment I was too desperate to stop myself from taking advantage of him.

Inspector Keen was waiting for us to finish our greetings. After a while he cleared his throat, asking, "Is this man your lawyer?"

I pulled myself out of Bryan's arms. "Yes." Then I introduced them. "Inspector Keen, this is Bryan Hancock, my lawyer. Bryan — Inspector Keen."

While this was happening, Dan Brewster had been standing to one side, after getting out of one of the police cars. As we walked into the police station, I gave Bryan a quick briefing about Jack's murder. He was shocked, and appalled that I hadn't contacted him immediately, as soon as I'd discovered Jack. That was something I couldn't even explain to myself, so how could I explain it to him? The truth of the matter was that I hadn't even thought about him until Dan Brewster had asked me if I didn't have a lawyer.

During the proceedings in the police station I noticed Dan glaring at Bryan. He was making it very apparent that he didn't like him. And remembering that he had read Jack's letter telling me *he* didn't like him, it was understandable. But Bryan was a very astute lawyer, and after he heard the entire story, which came out in a jumble, he argued that someone else could have used the paper knife and not left any fingerprints on it, because he or she had worn gloves. That deduction wasn't too clever, but he had a way with words and a courtroom manner that made everything he said sound important.

After he'd had his say, Dan was questioned and told about my having had the paper knife in my hands earlier that evening; not only that, but since the knife was part of the furnishings of my desk, naturally my fingerprints would be on it.

The result was that I wasn't booked at that time for the murder of Sylvia. I think Inspector Keen and the desk sergeant were still suspicious of me, but they couldn't actually prove anything. So we were all released but told to keep ourselves available for further questioning.

When we were all out on the sidewalk, Dan came over to me and said, "Well, good night, Mrs. Evers. I guess you won't need me any more tonight."

Bryan had hold of my arm, and I looked up at Dan in surprise. "But I thought you were going to spend the night at the house?"

Bryan said, "What? Are you crazy, Amelia? From what I've heard in there —" he jerked his head toward the police station — "you scarcely know this fellow. And there are legal aspects connected with Jack's death. I'm your lawyer. It's *my* duty to look after you. You should have called me earlier."

That I couldn't deny, but it annoyed me to have him say it. I pulled my arm from his possessive grasp. "Oh, Bryan!" I snapped. "Stop trying to run my life for me. You take care of the legal end of things and let me handle the rest of it. Please!"

"But —" he began.

"But nothing. Thank you for helping me in there." I indicated the police station with a nod of my head. "I'll get in touch with you."

His jaw tightened. He wasn't one to give up easily. He said, "You've got to find Jack's will."

"Oh, Bryan!" I sighed with exasperation. "Jack's only been gone for a few hours!"

"But you've got to find his will!" he persisted. "You won't know how you stand until you do."

This was too much, out there on the street, with the cold, icy wind blowing around us. "His lawyer probably has it," I snapped, and held out a cold hand to Dan, saying, "Please, Dan, Althea and I don't want to be alone in that house, with just those policemen."

Bryan grabbed my arm. "Amelia, have you lost your mind!" he cried. "You can't let this man stay with you. If you feel you need protection, I'll stay with you. Don't you read the papers? Don't you know what happens to people these days? How can you pick up a strange man and ask him to spend the night in your house?"

For a moment I didn't know whether I was going to laugh or cry. "And suppose *you* spent the night in the house, who would protect me from *you?*" I asked him. "Besides, Althea makes a perfect chaperone." I gave him a smile and patted his cheek. "Good night, Bryan," I said. "And thanks for coming over. I'll call you." Then, turning to Dan, I said, "Here comes a taxi. Let's grab it."

Chapter Five

We were in the taxi, being whisked away from the angry Bryan, when Dan said, "Perhaps you shouldn't have done that."

"What?"

"Treated your friend like that."

"Perhaps I shouldn't. He is really a darling, and he has been very good to me since I've been alone. But sometimes he gets terribly bossy. And sometimes — well, I'm afraid he likes me too much."

"And you don't like him?"

"Not that way."

He let it go at that and changed the subject, asking, "How is your aunt taking all the excitement?"

"She's upset, of course. When I was getting her to bed, just before we came out, she kept talking about one of the imaginary characters who people her world."

"It must be very trying for you."

"Oh, I don't mind. I'd really miss her if she ever had to be put into a sanitarium."

When we reached the house, we found the press had arrived, and we had to push our way through the cluster of both men and women. With an arm around me, Dan helped me make it to the front door. But we couldn't avoid the clicking cameras or the called questions that were hurled at us from all sides. But finally, with the aid of the police, we made it inside, and the door was closed and locked. Inside, it was quiet. Sylvia's corpse was gone, and everything was cleaned up. I called to Althea and suggested we all go to bed, and she agreed willingly. But first I asked Dan if he would take the dog out in the back yard, as he couldn't go into the street because of the reporters. Althea said the dog had been very good all evening, staying up in my room and only giving a low growl if anyone went upstairs.

When Dan and Boy came back, I heard a policeman tell Dan they were going to be around all night; a couple in the kitchen, a couple out front, and one in the back yard. And after the last murder, a couple on the roof, although the skylight had been found hooked just the way Inspector Keen said he'd left it.

The fire was still burning in the living room, but there was a wire screen in front of it, so sparks couldn't do any damage, and we decided to leave it as it was. It would burn itself out before long. Dan, Althea, Boy and myself went up to bed. On the way upstairs,

Althea said, "Miss Amelia, can't I sleep in that little room on the second floor tonight? I don't want to be way up on the top floor all alone, now Miss Edna is down with you."

"Of course," I told her. "Bring your things down. You can sleep in that small room at the back side of the guest room where Mr. Brewster will be."

Dan said, "How about calling me Dan? You did in front of the police station."

I said, "All right," and avoided the look Althea gave me. She walked to the foot of the stairs to the third floor, then hesitated, looking up into the darkness. I asked, "Would you like us to go up with you?"

She nodded. "Yes, I would. I don't mind telling you — I'm scared."

So Dan and I went up with her. While she was in her room assembling her night things, I showed Dan Aunt Edna's room. It really was practically a museum piece, and I knew it would interest him.

His first reaction to it as I pushed open the door and snapped on a light was a low whistle. Then he said, "It's fantastic. It looks like a stage set for an early American play."

I said, "Yes, it does."

"It could have been lifted from George Washington's house at Mount Vernon."

Then, glancing around, "But I can see there are also things from a later period."

I said, "Yes," to that too.

In the far corner there was a glass cabinet. He walked over to it. In it were old coins, fans and various figurines. After examining the contents of the cabinet, he turned to an inlaid table nearby on which there was a collection of snuff boxes, antique jewelry, old china and even a handful of old lucifer matches, the kind they used back around 1835. These indeed were rare. They were three or four inches long and heaped on a china tray.

The room was furnished as a living room, with a fireplace at one end. But at the other, on a sort of dais, was the gilt bed with a draped canopy in which Aunt Edna slept.

Hanging from the center of the ceiling was a large crystal chandelier, and the light from the table lamp I'd lit when we entered the room struck the glass prisms so they shone with rainbow colors.

"Fantastic!" Dan said again. "I've never seen anything like it. Thank you for showing it to me."

I said, "Tomorrow you will meet Aunt Edna."

We heard Althea stirring in her room at the other end of the hall, and we left Aunt

Edna's room and went into the hall to wait for her. In a moment Althea joined us. "All right," she said. "I guess I was kind of slow."

We returned to the second floor, and I said, "Althea, after I've soaked my ankle in Epsom salts, will you bandage it for me?"

Before she could answer, Dan said, "Would you let me do it? I learned a lot of first aid during my years around oil wells."

I said, "Thanks. But I'm sure Althea can do it quite well."

He bowed. "Then I'll say good night."

I said, "Good night. If you want anything, call Althea. The bathroom is that middle door along the hall."

After Althea had fixed my ankle and gone to bed, I lay thinking. Sleep just wouldn't come. After a while I heard Althea begin to snore, so I knew she was asleep. Dan was still moving around in his room, and I could smell cigarette smoke. I looked over at Aunt Edna. She was asleep and snoring gently. Boy was asleep over by a window.

Suddenly I just had to get up. There were some letters of Jack's I decided I'd better burn so the police wouldn't find them. They were in the safe. I got up quietly, put on a long white quilted robe and white satin slippers, got the letters and tiptoed down the stairs. There was still some fire burning in the fireplace in the dropped living room, and an occasional crackle from one of the logs; otherwise everything was quiet on that floor.

I hurried down the two steps and across the room, set aside the screen and dropped to my knees before the fire. My hair was hanging loose around my shoulders, and I pushed it back. I didn't have to read any of the letters before I threw them into the fire, because I knew them by heart, as I did all of the letters Jack had ever written me.

Suddenly I had an urge to glance over my shoulder. I felt a presence, even though I hadn't heard anything. Dan was standing at the top of the two steps between the wrought-iron railings. He had on a maroon dressing gown over gray pajamas, and his dark brown hair was mussed as if he'd been running his fingers through it. My heart quavered. I said, "Oh, it's you. I couldn't sleep." Quickly I tossed the last letter into the flames, which were burning higher now, having been fed by my last letter from Jack.

Dan came down into the room and strode over to me, helping me to my feet, his eyes taking notice of my loosely hanging hair. "You shouldn't be down here alone at this time of night," he told me.

"But the house is well guarded," I reminded him.

He said, "Yes, I know." Then, looking deeply into my eyes, "I want you to feel I'm your friend, Amelia." His nearness was disturbing to me, and I wondered why. When I didn't say anything, he began to speak again. "I don't believe you killed Sylvia," he said. "But you're in a tight spot. And unless we can discover the real murderer, it may be bad for you."

I nodded. "I realize that."

"Then you'll have to trust me enough to confide in me." He glanced at Jack's last letter crumbling to black wafers and disintegrating upon the burning logs.

I gave him a quick look. I hoped there was no fright in it.

He said, "I mean, if you'd just tell me what you and Sylvia talked about, other than what you told the police, and what you were burning just now."

I began to feel tense. "I'd rather not."

"But how can I help you if I don't know all the facts?"

I pulled away from his hands, which were holding my arms. "Perhaps you couldn't help me, even if you did know."

"Are you going to tell your lawyer everything?"

"Bryan? Heavens no!"

"But, Amelia, you *must!*"

I looked him straight in the eyes. "The real facts would convict me even quicker than the circumstantial evidence."

He pulled me down on the sofa beside him. "Tell me about Aunt Edna," he said, suddenly changing the subject. "That room of hers is rather surprising."

I said, "Yes, isn't it?" Then I sighed. "Poor Aunt Edna. Her life has been so terribly tragic." Suddenly I wanted to talk, to tell this strange, kindly man everything.

He asked, "Could she have — ?"

"No, no," I said quickly, interrupting him. "She isn't that kind of crazy. She has delusions she is living back in the early eighteen hundreds. She was always a great student of early American history, and she was on the stage for years, until she was taken sick."

He asked, "Should I have heard of her?"

"Well, she is Edna Hilton Julliard."

He raised an eyebrow. "Yes, I've heard of her. And come to think of it, there was some tragedy connected with her."

I began to clasp and unclasp my hands in my lap. I guess I was more nervous than I realized. I said, "Yes. She saw my father killed. They were in the same show together. It was called, *A Friend of Washington*. There was a large crystal chandelier, like the one in her room. It was at the end of the last act that it happened. My father was standing beneath the chandelier. He was Washington. Aunt Edna was leaning against the mantel over the fireplace a few feet away. Suddenly, without warning, the chandelier crashed. My father crumpled beneath it. His skull was fractured. He never spoke or moved after the thing hit him."

Dan's brow puckered, and he shook his head sympathetically. "How awful!" he said. "Was it an accident?"

"Oh yes. It was just a faulty job of wiring. The show had changed theaters that week, and things had been set up in sort of a hurry. Ever since, Aunt Edna has lived in the period of that play. I finally had her room fixed to duplicate the stage set, except for the bed; that was in a French play she did before the Washington story."

Dan said, "It is surprising she would want a duplicate of the chandelier in her room."

"Yes, it is. But when the room was furnished, we didn't put it in, and she used to ask for it. She seems to have completely forgotten what happened that night on the stage; that is, as far as my father being killed is concerned. It's as if she rejects everything but her life before and up to the moment of the accident."

"Is that the entire story?" Dan asked. I had the feeling he didn't believe I'd told him everything.

I said, "Yes, except — well, Aunt Edna was very much in love with my father."

He seemed surprised at that. "Did your mother know?"

"I think so."

"And your father, was he in love with your aunt?"

"I think he was. She was very attractive. My mother and my father and Aunt Edna were in the same show together at the time of the tragedy."

"How did your mother take it?"

"She was shocked, of course. But she was never as sensitive a person as Aunt Edna, nor as romantic."

"Did your mother and Aunt Edna ever have any trouble about your father?"

"Oh, no. It was never anything that came out into the open. It was just one of those things that existed, with everybody pretending it didn't."

"And were you at the theater when the tragedy happened?"

"No. I was away at school."

For a few minutes we sat in silence, watching the variegated colors in the dying flames coming from the now skeletal logs.

Then I shivered, got up and put the screen before the fire. "And now," I said, "it's very late, and I'm tired and a little cold. Shall we go back to bed?" Silly of me, but all of a sudden I became conscious we were both in our nightclothes.

Dan stood up beside me, gazing at me as I watched the shadows and lights the flickering fire made across his face. He said, "I wish you'd tell me what you were burning when I came downstairs."

His probing made me angry. "If you are going to pry," I said crossly, "I'm afraid I shall have to ask you to leave my house." I turned and left the room, going up the two steps to the hall, then up the flight of stairs to the second floor. My ankle was hurting, and I had to limp a little, which rendered it difficult to make a dignified exit.

Dan followed me silently. In the upper hall, we parted with a whispered, "Good night," to each other, and on Dan's part, a last lingering look at my loosely hanging hair.

Chapter Six

Except for Aunt Edna, we were all awake early the next morning. I let her sleep late. I was standing looking out of one of the living room windows when Dan came downstairs. I thought he looked tired. He said, "Good morning. How do you feel?"

I turned from the window. "All right. And you?"

"Fine." Then, "I had an idea."

"What?"

"About the grocery boy. I was thinking that instead of going looking for him, it might be a better idea just to let him make a routine delivery of groceries this morning. I suppose the story will break in the morning papers, but if we are lucky, no one will have mentioned the grocery boy."

I said, "No, they didn't. At least *The Times* didn't." I indicated the paper I'd left on the sofa after skimming through it. We always had it delivered.

Dan said, "Shall I call Inspector Keen and talk to him about it?"

"If you want to."

So Dan went back to the sitting room and

called the inspector. "I'm not trying to interfere with whatever your plans are," he told him. "But I had this idea." He outlined the plan, and Inspector Keen agreed it was a good idea. So about nine o'clock I phoned my order, and Dan and I went down to the dining room to wait, eating a leisurely breakfast as we did so. The policemen who had been on duty all night had been replaced, and in a few minutes Inspector Keen arrived and waited in the butler's pantry, out of sight.

It wasn't too long a wait. Dan and I talked about this and that, but neither of us mentioned our meeting in the firelight. Dan had brought *The Times* down with him, and one of the policemen had brought in *The News*. We read both papers to pass the time. There was an account of our two murders, the fact that Jack and I were divorced. A picture of Dan with his arm around me was on the front page of *The News*, and *The Times* had the picture of Jack that had been in the living room. I hadn't noticed it was gone, and it made me furious to think one of the reporters or one of the policemen would have taken it without asking me. I asked Althea if any of the reporters had gotten into the house, and she said, "Yes. One. But I chased him out with the broom."

Surprisingly enough, the papers had the facts right. My heart was heavy as I read about Jack's untimely death, and the suspicions the police had of me in the connection with the murder of Sylvia. They hadn't found a picture of her so far.

Dan and I tried to talk about shows to distract us, but he had been in the city such a short time he didn't really know anything about the new plays. For a while we just sat and smoked and thought our own thoughts.

At ten-thirty the grocer's panel truck drove up and stopped in front of the house, and Nikki jumped out, got a carton of groceries from the back of the truck, came down the areaway steps and rang the bell. I was sitting at the end of the table facing the windows, and Dan was sitting at my left, facing the hallway.

Nikki was always whistling. This morning it was, "Raindrops are falling on my head." He was about thirty, rather nice-looking, of medium height, with dark curly hair, stocky and strong. His face was round and his skin sallow. He moved with the litheness of a cat.

We waited for Althea to shuffle along the hall to open the door and gate for him. Then we heard her say, "Oh, it's you, Nikki."

Nikki stopped whistling and said, "Sure. Who did you think it was — Santa Claus?"

Then he followed her along to the kitchen, carrying the carton of groceries: bread, milk, the usual things.

"Is he the regular delivery man?" Dan whispered to me.

I nodded.

We sat still and listened, waiting for the inspector to make a move. First we heard the sounds of the groceries being unloaded onto the kitchen table. Then Inspector Keen went into action. He walked out into the kitchen. "Good morning," he said.

Nikki said, "Good morning, sir."

Keen said, "You know there were two murders committed in this house yesterday?"

"Yes, sir. I'm sorry, sir."

As I listened, I tried to detect hidden meanings in Nikki's voice.

Keen asked, "What's your name?"

"Nicholas Radzinski."

"Polish?"

"No, sir. Hungarian."

"Naturalized citizen?"

"I was born in this country. My parents were born in Hungary."

"They living?"

"No, sir."

"Address?"

He gave a number on upper First Avenue.

Then the inspector said, "You were in this house yesterday afternoon."

"Yes, sir. But —"

"Just a minute!" Keen snapped at him. "Can you account for all of your time yesterday afternoon?"

"Yes, sir. I was on the route, delivering groceries until six o'clock."

"How can you prove it?"

"Why, I don't know. I just went from one house to the other. You can ask my boss. I was back in the store at the usual time."

Did I detect a slight nervousness in his voice, or was I just imagining it?

Dan was watching me. I whispered, "I can't see why *he* would have anything to do with it."

Dan just shrugged.

Keen asked, "Do you mind going over to headquarters and letting us take your fingerprints?"

Nikki hesitated. Then he said, "Why, no, sir." This time I was sure his voice shook a little. But whose wouldn't?

The inspector had made it sound like a polite request, but Nikki knew it was a definite order.

As he and Keen went by the dining room door, Nikki glanced in. First he looked at me; then his eyes met Dan's, and for a split-second I thought I saw a flaring hatred in his for both of us. Then he was gone, and I decided what I'd seen was probably only fright. I said, "I think it's a shame to scare that poor man by fingerprinting him. There's no earthly reason why he should have killed Jack or that girl."

Dan said, "Probably not."

We sat and talked for another half-hour or so but got nowhere. Dan Brewster was a very attractive and charming man, but I was in no frame of mind that morning to be affected by him. There was a barrier between us — Jack. And even though he had been very kind to me and was doing everything he could to help me, I kept thinking that I didn't really know anything about him.

Finally he said, "I think I'd better go to my hotel and see if there are any messages from my office."

I said, "All right. I guess I'll do a little dusting and help Althea. She's too upset to do much today." So Dan went up to his room for his hat and coat, and I got a duster and went up to dust the dropped living room.

I heard Dan meet Aunt Edna in the second floor hall, and I stopped to listen. Aunt Edna asked, "Did the President send you?" She still had the full, rich-bodied quality in her voice that she used to have back in the days when she was on the stage. I've always tried to copy it, but I don't think my timbre quite equals hers. "Tell him," she said, "that I helped his messenger get away last night. He used the skylight to the roof, and I gave him some of my special matches so he could see when he got up there."

I peeked up the stairs and saw Dan bow from the waist in a most courtly manner. "You did right, madam," he said. "And His Honor sends you his kindest regards and thanks and hopes you are well this fine morning."

Aunt Edna smiled, evidently pleased. She was still a very handsome woman, and when she talked her face became animated and very alive. This morning her face was beautiful. Her features were clearly defined; a long rather pointed nose, a large but well shaped mouth; cheeks with definite planes, a high forehead, clear penetrating blue eyes. Her hair had been black but was now a lovely silvery gray, but her straight brows were still black and were a startling contrast to her hair and eyes.

This morning, when Althea had helped her dress, she'd put on her housecoat of light blue which, like all the clothes I had a seamstress make for her, conformed to the current style, yet still was reminiscent of Colonial days.

Dan was telling her, "Your message will be delivered, madam."

Aunt Edna nodded regally, turned and went up the stairs to the third floor, and Dan went into his room for his things. When he came downstairs a few minutes later, I said, "I heard your meeting with Aunt Edna."

"Yes, we met in the hall. She's quite a character."

"Thank you for playing the game with her."

He smiled, and a kindly expression came into his eyes. "Could anyone do differently?"

I turned away and flipped the duster over a lamp shade so he wouldn't notice the tears that came to my eyes. I asked, "Will you be back for lunch?"

"I doubt it. I'll call you later."

I watched him run quickly down the brownstone stoop and dash into the street to hail a taxi. He was just missed by a panel truck — the one Nikki drove for the grocery store. I looked after it as it sped away. It could have been a coincidence that it was coming through our street again, but I didn't think so. It had seemed to head deliberately for Dan. But it was hard to believe that Nikki could do a thing like that. Then I remembered the look of hate in his eyes that morning. And now this.

But who was Nikki Radzinski? How was he mixed up in things? Why would he have killed Jack? And then Sylvia? Was I in danger? Or Ronny? Or Aunt Edna? Or Althea?

During the day I tried not to worry. But how could I help it? Gradually it dawned on me that if anything happened to Dan Brewster, I would feel very badly about it. In spite of my telling myself at breakfast that he was having no effect on me, I now had to admit that I was beginning to like him quite a lot.

Chapter Seven

It was after nine in the evening when Dan called me, but I was so relieved to hear from him I didn't complain.

He said, "Sorry I wasn't able to call you until now. Are you all right?"

I said, "Yes, yes, I'm fine. Are you all right?"

He said, "Yes."

"Have you had dinner?"

He hesitated. "No, come to think of it, I haven't. Nor any lunch either. I've been busy."

"Well, for goodness sakes!" I cried. "Come on over, or up, or down, depending on where you are, and I'll have Althea fix you something."

He said, "Be there in a few minutes." Then — I could have imagined it — but I thought I heard him say, "You darling," under his breath. But of course I could have been mistaken. Anyway, he'd hung up.

I called down to Althea, who was still in the kitchen, and asked her to make some chicken salad sandwiches and coffee and bring them up to the living room, explaining why I wanted anything that time in the evening. The rest of us had eaten dinner at six.

When Dan arrived, I opened the door myself, holding Boy by the collar. There was a plain-clothes man posted across the street. It was the one who had come with Inspector Keen yesterday, so I knew he would recognize Dan.

I had a cheery fire in the living room fireplace, and Althea had brought up a plate of sandwiches and a pot of coffee a few minutes before.

Dan put his hat and coat on a chair, but not the same one where he'd put them yesterday. He was still wearing the hat with the cut in it, but he'd fixed it so the cut wasn't too visible.

I said, "You must be starved. Come and sit by the fire. I hope this is enough for you?" I indicated the food on the low table.

He sat down beside me on the sofa. "It looks wonderful," he said, "and so do you."

I was wearing a green plaid jumper over a long-sleeved yellow blouse, and I had piled my hair on top of my head. "Thank you," I said, flushing a little, and began to serve him the food and poured out a cup of coffee.

"Now then," I said, "tell me what you've been doing. Or isn't it any of my business?"

He said, "Yes, I think it *is* your business."

He took a bite out of a sandwich. "To begin with, I went down to see my boss. I knew he would see my picture in the papers and read the account of the happenings here. Then, too, he was Jack's boss."

I said, "Yes, I know. What did he say?"

"Well, I told him the whole story, and he was very sympathetic and wanted me to extend to you his sympathy and tell you that if there was anything he could do, he would be glad to."

I said, "That's nice of him."

"He's a prince of a fellow. But to make a long story short, when I offered to resign, he refused to accept my resignation."

I said, "Oh, Dan, you didn't!"

He shrugged. "I felt it was the only thing to do, considering that Jack and I were both employees of the company. But he said just to forget it, and when things quieted down I could go back down to South America or stay here in the office as a consultant, if I wanted to."

I couldn't speak at the moment because of the lump in my throat, so Dan went on, "Well, after I left the office, I went up to my hotel. I was kind of tired, and I guess I didn't sleep much last night."

"Who did?"

He smiled. "Well, Althea, for one. Or if

she didn't, she snores when she's awake."

I smiled, and he continued his story. "When I got to the hotel, I took off my hat, overcoat, suit coat, tie and shoes and threw myself down on the bed. I guess I went right to sleep. After a while I was awakened by the phone ringing. I rolled over, reached for it and said, 'Yes? Brewster speaking.' A man's voice said, 'If you want information about the murders at the Evers place, come to —' He gave me an address on First Avenue. It sounded familiar. I remembered it was the one Nikki had given Inspector Keen that morning."

I interrupted him. "Dan, did he try to run you down this morning, when you left here and went out into the street to hail a cab?"

He looked surprised. "Why, no. That is, I don't think so. Some car or truck grazed me, but I got out of the way just in time."

We looked at one another questioningly, and I said, "It was Nikki in the grocery truck. Apparently they didn't keep him very long at the police station. I was at the window and saw the whole thing."

Dan took another bite of sandwich. "Well," he said, "if it was Nikki, I'm sure it was an accident. I shouldn't have run out into the traffic the way I did."

"Well, go on with your story."

"Okay. So I asked the man on the phone if he was Nikki Radzinski. But whoever it was said, 'I'm not answering questions. Be at the address at eight o'clock. Top floor rear. And come alone. Don't tell the police.' Then there was a click, and he was gone. I knew it was hopeless to try to trace the call. I looked at my watch. It was seven-thirty. I'd slept nearly all afternoon, and I was hungry. But there was no time for food. By the time I took a shower, shaved and put on fresh clothing, I'd just have time to make my First Avenue appointment by eight o'clock.

"Naturally, I wondered if I was walking into a trap. If Nikki was the murderer, was he out to get me? I didn't have a weapon of any sort and decided against telling our friend Keen about my invitation.

"The address was near One Hundredth Street. I walked over to First Avenue and hopped a bus. When I reached there, I gave a quick look around. There was a barbershop, several second-hand shops, small dingy grocery stores, mostly foreign. But the only place open at that time of night was the barber's. I regretted having shaved. Barbers are usually excellent sources of information about the neighbors. But it was too late to worry about that.

"I looked at the numbers. The one I

wanted was in the middle of the block. It was a rickety old building, lit only by dim, uncovered light bulbs in the hall ceiling. I went in and looked at the names on the mail boxes. Radzinski was at the end of the row."

I cried, "Then it *was* Nikki!"

He nodded. "Yes. I rang the bell beneath the name. After a moment there was a clicking sound, and the door to the hall was released so I could enter. The hall was dingy and smelly, and the stairs were steep and narrow. I went up four flights. On the top floor a door at the back opened, and Nikki stood framed in the doorway, a dim flickering light silhouetting his thick body against a sparsely furnished room. When he saw me he looked surprised. 'What do *you* want?' he snapped.

"I said, 'You invited me to visit you at eight o'clock, didn't you?' 'Are you crazy?' he asked. We stared at each other. I said, 'Not yet.' Then I asked, 'May I come in?' He stepped aside, and I walked through the doorway into what was evidently a one-room, cold water flat. There was a table, a couple of broken chairs and an unmade single bed. In one corner was a battered-looking trunk with clothes tumbling out of it. On one end the name RADZINSKI was stenciled in red. It looked like a theatrical trunk. I've often seen them at railroad terminals. Through a dirty, cracked window I could see a fire escape. I said, 'You ever on the stage?'

"His body stiffened, and his dark eyes watched me. His mouth tightened, and I had the feeling that at any moment he might jump me. I'd brought him a carton of cigarettes, and I handed it to him, saying, 'Hope these are your brand.' He took the carton and tossed it on the unmade bed, not answering my question. I said, 'I asked you if you were ever on the stage?' 'Who wants to know?' he snapped.

"I offered him a cigarette from a pack I had in my pocket, and he took it. Then I took out my lighter, and we leaned together as I held the light for him. I noticed that his hand was shaking and he was breathing heavily. I also noticed there was no phone in the room, if I needed help in a hurry.

"After I lit my own cigarette, I asked, 'May I sit down?' He said, 'Sure,' and we each sat down on a chair. I said, 'Okay, now let's have it. Where do you fit into that mess down at the Evers' house?'

"He gave me that ugly look I'd seen in his eyes as he passed the dining room door here this morning."

I interrupted him. "Then you noticed it,

too? I wasn't sure."

He said, "Yes, I noticed it. It was unmistakable. But let me go on with my story. He answered my question by saying, 'How would I know anything about the murders? Just because I deliver groceries there, is that any reason why I should know anything about what goes on there?'

"I looked at him through the cloud of smoke that was accumulating in the small room. I asked, 'Then why did you phone me at my hotel a little while ago and tell me if I came here at eight o'clock, I'd learn something about the murders?'

"He said, 'I didn't!'

"I tried to keep my temper. 'Then who did?' I asked him. He said, 'How should I know?'

" 'Look, Nikki,' I said. 'I don't know how you're mixed up in this, but if you know anything about it, I wish you'd tell me or the police. Did you ever know any of the Evers family in the theater?'

" 'No!' he yelled. 'We weren't in the same line.'

"I felt I'd struck oil. 'Then you *were* in the theater?' I nodded at the trunk.

"He jumped up and kicked over his chair. 'So what if I was?' he yelled at me.

"I pretended not to notice his agitation. I

asked, 'What did you do? Sing? Dance?'

" 'Neither,' he said more quietly. 'My wife and I had an act together.'

"I felt I was making headway. I said, 'Oh, why did you give it up?'

"He began to pace back and forth in the small room, his face white. He threw his cigarette on the floor and stepped on it; then he stood defiantly in front of me. 'Because my wife walked out on me. She thought she could do better on her own!' He practically spat the words at me.

" 'I'm sorry,' I said. 'I didn't mean to touch a sore spot.'

"He picked up the kicked-over chair and collapsed on it. 'It isn't sore — any more.'

"I offered him another cigarette, and he took it, letting me hold the lighter for him. I asked, 'Was that when you went into the grocery store?' Then he said, 'No. I've only been with the grocery store six months.'

" 'And before that?'

" 'I volunteered for the Army. Got a quickie training and then shipped over to Vietnam.'

" 'Were you there long?'

"He smiled ruefully. 'No. I got hit in the head the first week I was there, and they shipped me over to Hawaii to a hospital, then home.'

"Then I asked him, 'Did you get a medical discharge?'

" 'That's right,' he said.

" 'Your head all right now?' I asked.

"He said, 'Most of the time. Sometimes I get headaches and —' He shrugged.

"I kept at him, asking, 'Do you have to report to an army doctor about your head?'

" 'Not any more,' he said. 'They say the headaches will stop — some day?'

"I asked, 'And as soon as you were discharged, did you get the job at the grocery store?'

"He said, 'No. I was a short order clerk in a luncheonette for a while.'

"I persisted. 'And did your wife make good on her own?'

"His mouth twisted to one side in an ugly leer. 'Yeah,' he said, 'she did all right. She really did all right.' It was plain to see he was very bitter.

"I asked, 'Is she still your wife, legally?'

"Again he jumped up, but this time he didn't kick over the chair. 'What the devil are you trying to find out?' he yelled at me. 'What business is it of yours whether or not my wife is still married to me or not? Why don't you get the blazes out of here and let me alone?' He was very upset, and his voice sounded choked as he went on. 'A guy tries to make an honest living, and what happens? Somebody gets murdered, and just because a guy delivers groceries to the house he gets fingerprinted and loses his job!'

"I got to my feet and faced him. I wasn't too proud of myself for probing into his life. But somehow I felt I'd unearthed something. I wasn't quite sure what, but I'd sort it out later.

"I asked, 'How did you lose your job? Not just because the police took your fingerprints?'

"He glared at me, and I could feel his hot breath on my face. He'd been eating garlic. 'Yes,' he snapped, 'just because the police took my fingerprints. It got around the neighborhood, and the dames got scared. A lot of 'em called the boss and said they wouldn't let me in the house any more. So I got fired.' He took a step nearer me and yelled, 'And now get out!'

"I shrugged and turned to go. What else could I do? I said, 'All right, Nikki. I'm sorry about your job. If you need money, I'll be glad to lend you some until you get another job.' Somehow he looked forlorn, standing there in the shabby room, his belligerence now seeming to be seeping out of him.

"I opened the door, but he said, 'Hey, wait a minute!'

"So I turned around. The ugly look had left his face, and a bland, childish look had replaced it. 'Just who are *you*, anyway?' he asked me.

"I didn't know exactly how to answer that, but I said, 'My name is Dan Brewster. I'm an oil man — engineer.' He waited for me to say more, so I added 'I'm on a vacation. And I'm a friend of Mrs. Evers.'

"He looked at me thoughtfully for a while; then he asked, 'How do I know *you* didn't commit the murders yourself?'

"Our eyes met. I said, 'You don't. And I don't know whether you did or not. So we're even on that score.'

"Then he asked me another question. 'Where do you work, when you aren't on vacation?'

"I told him, 'I've been down in Venezuela for a couple of years. I don't know whether I'll be sent back there or kept here in the New York office for a while.'

"He gave me a questioning look, but before he could ask any more questions I said, 'Well, I guess I'll be running along. If I can do anything for you, you can reach me at my hotel.'

"He asked, '*What* hotel?'

"I decided that either he was a very clever actor or he really wasn't the man who had phoned me. I told him the name of my hotel and went out. I was down on the street when I remembered that the name of my hotel had been given in the papers, along with the rest of the story."

Dan ate another bite of sandwich before he went on with his story. Then he said, "Well, by that time it was nearly nine o'clock. But the barber shop was still open. I decided I'd get a haircut. I didn't really need one, but I wanted to have a visit with the barber. When I was settled in the chair, I asked, 'How's business?'

"He clipped at my hair. 'Oh, business is okay.'

"I asked, 'Know many of your neighbors around here?'

"He said, 'Yeah, I know most of 'em.'

"I decided he wasn't the talkative type. But I kept trying. I said, 'I was just up to see a friend of mine — Nikki Radzinski.'

"His face brightened. 'Oh, Nikki. He's a nice boy.'

" 'Yes,' I agreed. 'But he seems a bit nervous.'

"He nodded. 'Yeah, something's eatin' him. His wife walked out on him a few years ago, so the story goes. And then he joined the Army and got a head injury. Gets awful headaches. But outside of that he's a nice fellow.'

"I couldn't think of any more questions to ask and he had finished my hair, which hadn't needed trimming in the first place. So I paid him, and gave him a generous tip and said, 'Well, so long. See you again sometime.' And I went out. I walked downtown until I found a drugstore with a phone booth and called you."

I said, "Oh Dan, I've been worried about you all day."

In answer he took my hand and gripped it.

Chapter Eight

Dan's story had been long, and for a while I just sat thinking about it. Finally I said, "Poor Nikki, I wish I could help him. It was ridiculous to haul him off to the police station that way." I poured myself some coffee, while Dan began to eat another sandwich. Putting down the coffeepot, I said, "I could give him some work here for a while. The windows all need washing, and the Venetian blinds could stand a good cleaning."

"But you don't know anything about him," Dan protested. "Suppose he *did* have something to do with — ?"

"But that's ridiculous!" I argued. "He's only the grocery boy." I nibbled at a sandwich, but I wasn't hungry. However, I did manage to do away with half of one.

"But he used to be on the stage. And he and his wife had an act together," Dan pointed out. "And he's very bitter about her walking out on him."

"If you're intimating his wife was Sylvia, your imagination is running away with you," I told him.

"I know it sounds crazy," he argued. "But it *could* be."

"Nonsense!" I cried. "They just aren't — weren't the same type at all."

Dan shrugged. "That's a silly reason."

"I don't care," I said. "I like Nikki, and I'm going up to his place in the morning and offer him some work. I can't help feeling personally responsible for his losing his job."

Dan poured himself some more coffee. "Before you do anything about him," he said, "promise me you'll talk it over with Inspector Keen first."

I sighed. "Oh, all right. But I think it's all perfectly silly."

Dan kept drinking coffee and eating sandwiches. "You people seem to like garlic," he said, looking at the sandwich he was eating.

"Garlic? I like a little as a flavoring."

Dan blew out his breath. "Whew!" he said. "It must be in the mayonnaise. And the chopped peppers are murder. My mouth is burning."

"Chopped peppers?" I asked. "We never use them. But these sandwiches do seem to be rather hot." I picked up half a one, took a bite of it and laid it down.

"Would you like some brandy?" I asked. Then I realized the bottle was in the hall closet, and for a moment I thought I was going to faint. After a few moments I said, "I'll have to get over remembering."

Dan said, "No thanks, anyway." Then he asked, "Why don't you close this house and go live with your mother for a while?"

I said, "No. I don't think I'd be happy with Mother. She has her own life, and Ronny makes her nervous. And she doesn't like Boy. She's trying to be the perfect grandmother now, but I know she'll be glad when I'm able to bring Ronny home. Besides, there's Aunt Edna. And Mother only has a small apartment. And if the police are going to come and poke around here every time they get a clue, I sort of like to be here to know what they're doing." I hadn't meant to let that last slip out, but it seemed to be a time for confidences.

"Were they here poking around today?" Dan asked.

"Oh yes."

"Did they find anything?"

"I don't think so. Besides, Bryan was here and took care of them." I hadn't meant to tell him that, either.

He said, "Oh? What was he doing here?"

"He came to talk business. He's my lawyer, remember?"

I guess I sounded annoyed, because he

said, "Yes, I remember," in a rather weary-sounding voice.

I said, "Jack's lawyer was here, too. He brought Jack's will."

"Was Bryan here when the other lawyer came?"

"Yes. I wish he hadn't been."

"You mean they don't get along?"

"Well, Mr. Wells is overly conservative, and a lot older than Bryan."

"Perhaps that makes him more experienced."

"You're probably right. But Bryan seemed experienced, too, and after we were divorced, I didn't want to have the same lawyer Jack had."

"Did you and Jack see much of Bryan before Jack went down to South America?"

"Not much. We met him at a cocktail party and used to get together once in a while."

"This may sound inquisitive and none of my business, but is Bryan financially comfortable?"

"What you really mean is — is he interested in me because maybe I have more money than he has?"

"Well, in a way, yes."

"I think I have. But it's not very flattering to suggest a man couldn't be interested in me because of myself."

"You know I don't mean that."

"Would you be?"

"If you remember, I became interested in you even before I met you. And at that time I knew nothing about your financial status, or Jack's. He never talked about money." After a moment he asked, "Did Mr. Wells read Jack's will before Bryan?"

"He didn't want to, but I told him it would be all right."

"Was Bryan satisfied with the contents of the will?"

"That's a strange question."

"What I mean is, was Sylvia mentioned in the will?"

"No. Strangely, she wasn't. It seems the will was made shortly after Jack and I were married, and he had never gotten around to changing it in Sylvia's favor."

"Was that what Bryan meant when he said, 'You've got to find Jack's will'?"

"Perhaps. Naturally, he is concerned about my welfare."

"Of course."

We sat silently for a while; then Dan asked, "Is there anything I can do to help? I mean if — well, Jack was probably giving you alimony. If that stops now and you should need some quick money, I can let you have some. I'm not exactly starving myself. I make a good salary, and my father left me fairly well off."

Quick tears came to my eyes, and I patted his arm. "You're a darling, Dan," I said. "But I'm in very good financial condition. My father left me something, too; and a grandmother, my father's mother, left me money a few years ago."

"And that is what Bryan is handling for you?"

"Yes."

"And Jack's will?"

"Left me everything. He knew I'd always take care of Ronny."

"Will you take all of Jack's affairs away from Mr. Wells now and turn them over to Bryan?"

"I don't know. That's what he wants me to do, of course. But —"

"But you are beginning to lose confidence in him?"

"A little."

"What does Mr. Wells suggest?"

"Nothing. He said he would do anything I wanted him to do?"

"But you know he doesn't approve of Bryan?"

"He doesn't like him personally. He has never expressed an opinion about his business ability."

Boy was lying with his forepaws on Dan's feet and his huge head on his forepaws. I knew he was very heavy and it must be uncomfortable for Dan. I said, "Boy seems to like you, but if he bothers you just push him away."

He leaned down and scratched Boy's ear. "He doesn't bother me. And I'm glad he does like me. I don't imagine it would be very healthy for anyone he didn't like." Then he returned to talking about my problem. "You could get a little place in the country," he suggested, "over on Long Island or up in Westchester or Connecticut."

I couldn't help smiling at his eagerness. "You're very kind to worry about me," I told him. "But I guess I'd better wait awhile. I may still be arrested for murder."

He gripped my hand hard. Suddenly I began to cry, and he took me into his arms. "Forgive me," he said. "I'm a clumsy, muddling fool. But everything is going to be all right. They'll find the guilty person, and you won't have to worry any more."

I managed to stop crying and pulled away from his comforting arms. "I have a confession to make," I told him.

He gave me his handkerchief, saying, "Please don't tell me anything you don't want to."

I dried my eyes and blew my nose. "But I *do* want to. You remember last night, when you came downstairs and I was burning something in the fireplace?" I gave him back his handkerchief, and he returned it to his pocket. "Yes," he said.

"Well, I was burning letters from Jack."

"The ones he read to me down in South America?"

"No. New ones. Ones he'd written since he returned to this country — since his marriage to Sylvia."

Dan sat quietly letting me tell it in my own way. I went on, "He discovered he'd made a mistake, that Sylvia wasn't what he'd thought she was. He wanted to divorce her and come back to me and Ronny."

Dan stared at me. I kept on talking. "But she wouldn't give him a divorce. I think she really loved him, and she liked the kind of life he was able to give her. And she was going to have a baby. That was why I gave her money. She said she needed some right away, and Jack had never given her any cash."

"Why didn't you tell the police that last night?"

"I couldn't. I don't know why, but I just couldn't."

"Would you have taken Jack back?"

I nodded.

Dan asked, "Why did you burn Jack's letters?"

"Why, so the police wouldn't find them, of course. They would have today, if I'd had them anywhere in the house. They went through everything, even made me open the safe I have in my bedroom. Can't you see? That's all they'd have needed to close the case: *Ex-wife rids herself of woman who wouldn't divorce the man she wanted to remarry.*"

He looked at me thoughtfully. "But you've forgotten that Jack was killed *before* Sylvia."

I tried to smile. "I guess I'm all mixed up — about everything," I said. "And I'm very sorry you had to be involved in it. If you'd rather not stay here tonight, it will be all right. There's a man guarding the house. And I have Boy."

Dan said, "Well, if you're sure you won't be nervous — my stomach seems to be kicking back at me, and I think I'd better go on over to my hotel. Keep Althea down on the floor with you."

"Yes, I will. As a matter of fact, she's already in bed. She fixed your supper, had some herself, then went to bed."

Dan said, "Well, thank her for mine. Everything was delicious. And now, if you're sure you'll be all right tonight, I'll run along. I'll leave my things until another time. They won't be in your way, will they?"

I assured him they wouldn't and accompanied him to the front door. Then, just before he went out, he asked, "Did you tell Bryan about those letters you burned?"

"No, of course not."

He patted my shoulder. "Well, good night," he said. "And be sure to call me if you should need me, or even if you just feel lonely and want to talk. I'll come up in the morning anyway." Then he gave me a long lingering look that made me feel so uneasy I had to say, "Dan, please don't get any ideas about me. I couldn't bear it."

He gently pinched my chin and said, "You're a sweet girl, Amelia. You don't mind if I think that, do you?"

What could I say but, "No, I guess not. See you tomorrow?"

Chapter Nine

But I didn't see him the next day, because during the night Althea and I were both taken sick. Our mouths burned, and we were terribly nauseated. I managed to phone our doctor, and he said it seemed to be food poisoning of some sort. Fortunately, our cases weren't serious. But when I saw the morning paper I was terribly upset by a headline that read:

MAN INVOLVED
IN EVERS MURDERS POISONED

Naturally, I wondered if there had been something wrong with those sandwiches Althea had made for us.

I didn't know until later what Dan was experiencing in the hospital. Inspector Keen had even accused him of trying to commit suicide. It seems we had all been made sick by phosphorus poisoning. They had even gone so far as to take the contents of our garbage can and have them analyzed. That was how they pinpointed it to our house; and Inspector Keen, when he found out

Althea and I had also been taken sick, came and questioned us unmercifully. He asked about Aunt Edna. Had she been sick? I said, "No." Then he began to ask about the bread the sandwiches had been made of, and it turned out the bread had only been used for the chicken salad sandwiches. Aunt Edna hadn't had any of them, and she never ate bread, anyway.

I called the hospital, but they wouldn't let me talk to Dan. And when I asked how he was, the telephone operator said, "He's getting along as well as can be expected." So there was nothing I could do but wait and worry.

Dan arrived the next day, looking kind of washed out. The first thing he said was, "I've just been to the public library, reading up on phosphorous poisoning."

I said, "Why?"

"Why?" he almost yelled at me. "Because we all were nearly killed by phosphorus poisoning!"

I said, "I'm sorry, Dan. Inspector Keen told me you were very ill, but Althea and I had just a touch of it, I guess because we didn't eat very much."

"And I made a pig of myself because I was hungry."

"Please, Dan, it was an accident."

"Was it?" We were sitting in the dropped

living room, I on the sofa and he in the cherry brocade chair. There was no fire in the fireplace.

"Do you want me to read you what I found in the library about phosphorus poisoning?" he demanded.

Without waiting for my answer, he took a piece of paper from a pocket and read:

. . . *White or yellow phosphorus is used in fireworks, rat poison, smoke screens, in gas analysis, and in manufacturing phosphoric acid. Lucifer matches originally had heads of white phosphorus, sand, potassium chlorate, glue, etc., and were ignited by friction; but because of the poisonous nature of white phosphorus their use was prohibited by law. . . .**

---

* From: POISONS, Their Properties, Chemical Identification, Symptoms, and Emergency Treatments. By: Vincent J. Brooks, Sergeant N. J. State Police, and Hubart N. Alyea, Associate Professor of Chemistry Princeton University. Published by: D. VanNostrand Company, New York.

He looked at me over the top of the paper. "*Lucifer matches!* Do you get the connection?"

I said, "No, I'm afraid I don't."

He folded the paper and returned it to his pocket. "You don't? Didn't you show me some very old lucifer matches up in Aunt Edna's room?"

"You mean — ?"

"I mean, the police found a nice sprinkling of white phosphorus in the bread those sandwiches were made of. It's very poisonous, and it was tucked into the little holes in the bread in such a clever way you'd never notice it, unless you were looking for it."

"But you can't think Althea would — ?"

"No, but your Aunt Edna told me she helped Washington's messenger get away. Maybe she gave him some of her lucifer matches so he could see his way around."

"Oh, for heaven sakes!" I exploded. "Anyone would think you'd been watching too many TV shows."

"Well, I haven't. And you mustn't give that Nikki a job here!"

"Nikki? How did you get him into it?"

"How did *I* get him into it?"

"Yes. I asked Inspector Keen about him yesterday, and he said as far as they could find out he was okay. His record is clean. He used to be with a traveling circus; then he went into the Army and got a head injury and was given a medical discharge. Then, as soon as he was well enough, he got a job as a short order clerk in a luncheonette — and the last six months he's been with the grocery store."

Dan leaned forward in his chair. "A traveling circus, you said?"

I nodded. "More like a traveling vaudeville show, I guess it was. Played small towns and fairs and had a tour through middle Europe one time. He was one of those knife throwers. You know, they juggle a couple of handfuls of knives for a while; then they stand a girl up against a board and outline her with knives they flip from the other side of the stage. You see them occasionally on TV specials."

Dan jumped to his feet and began pacing the floor; then he stopped beside me. "That's it!" he cried. "Can't you *see?* Knives! Knife thrower! Traveling show! Sylvia Sanderson! Sylvia Evers! He must be her ex-husband!"

"Who?"

"Nikki, of course!"

"You're crazy."

"No, I'm not. I'm going to call Keen." He started for the sitting room and the phone, but I stopped him. "You can't do that!" I cried. "To begin with, it doesn't add up. Besides, the police couldn't arrest him just because he was Sylvia's ex-husband, even if he is. They could question him, yes, but if he didn't want to talk he wouldn't. And they haven't any definite evidence against him. The knife that killed Jack hasn't been found; the one in your hat didn't have fingerprints; and the only fingerprints on the paper knife that killed Sylvia were mine."

He stopped, turned, stared at me, then came and sat down on the sofa beside me. With a big sigh he said, "You're right, of course. But just to please me, don't have Nikki here in the house to do anything."

"You're being silly," I told him. "I feel personally responsible for his losing his job, and I feel I owe him something."

So I wrote him a note and offered him work, and he gladly accepted. But Dan was worried about it, and when he told me he had lost his hotel room because of a convention that had booked all the rooms a long time ago, and asked if he could come back with me, I was a little suspicious of his story. I was sure it was just an excuse to get me to have him as a house guest again. And to tell the truth, I was glad to have him. So the first day Nikki started work with me, Dan moved in, bag and baggage.

We still had the inquest and funerals to go

through. But the inquest didn't reveal anything we didn't already know. And the funerals were private and were soon over. Then we all settled down to wait for Inspector Keen's next move.

Dan, I know, watched every move Nikki made. And so did Boy. I thought, Well, now we'll see. They say children and dogs are good judges of character. So I watched Boy when he was near Nikki. Boy followed him around like a shadow, and Nikki talked to him. Boy cocked his head to one side and listened. And it wasn't any time at all before they were the best of friends.

Althea still slept in the small room next to Dan's with an audibility that sometimes got on my nerves. And Aunt Edna was still sleeping in my room. She went up to her own room during the day, but at night I insisted she stay with me.

Bryan was in and out of the house from time to time, and whenever he and Dan met you could feel antagonism bristling between them. One day Bryan said to Dan, "Don't you think you've been hanging around here long enough?"

I could see his attitude annoyed Dan, and I wasn't surprised when Dan looked him straight in the eyes and said, "When I do, I'll pack up and go."

In the beginning, Dan and I had had an argument about his paying board. He had insisted it was only fair, and I had flatly refused to allow him to. So he compromised by bringing in big thick steaks, wine and liquors and exotic foods from out-of-the-way shops in the city.

As the days and the nights passed, the mystery deepened. It was like a puzzle, no pieces of which would fit. And the police didn't seem to be getting anywhere. If they were, they were keeping it to themselves. I thought and thought until my head seemed to spin like a top. There must be a clue somewhere we had all overlooked. Dan and I often discussed it but could arrive at no conclusion.

One day Dan said, "I've been thinking about your mother. She sounds like an interesting person. I'd like to meet her."

I was rather surprised. "Surely you don't suspect *her?*" I said.

"Of course not. I'd just like to meet her. After all, she *is* your mother."

"Yes, she is. Perhaps we could go up to her place for a while this afternoon, if she's going to be in." I phoned her, and she said she would be at home and invited us for tea. Ronny was still staying there, so I took him some extra clothing and a few of his toys.

When we arrived at Mother's, she was alone. She said the maid had taken Ronny for a walk, but they would be back soon.

I couldn't help but watch Dan's reaction to everything. Mother's apartment is in one of those impressive-looking doorman buildings with an awning over the entrance. The apartment itself is three rooms with a large living room which Mother has furnished tastefully and expensively; only to me it has always looked as if it were done by an interior decorator. Which it was. The personal touch is completely missing.

There is a small square entrance hall with an Oriental rug laid on the highly polished floor, one of those console tables with a mirror over it at one side, and a couple of straight-backed chairs on the other. Between the chairs is a door to a coat closet, and we hung our wraps there.

Mother greeted us pleasantly enough, after we'd disposed of our coats and the small bag I'd brought with Ronny's things, then ushered us into the living room. I never felt quite at home at Mother's, and I was wondering how Dan felt. I introduced them, and they bowed and shook hands. Then I said, "I brought some more clothes and toys for Ronny."

Mother looked annoyed. "How much

longer do I have to keep him here? You know the only place I have for him to sleep is on that day bed in my room."

I could feel myself tense. "Does he bother you?" I asked, I guess rather sharply. We were all standing in the middle of the living room by that time.

Mother said, "Of course he doesn't bother me. Mary takes full charge of him. I have too much else to do."

"Such as?" I asked her.

Mother's lips tightened. "Oh, don't be tiresome!" she snapped. "You know perfectly well I have my charities, which take a great deal of my time."

Tears came to my eyes, and I walked over and pretended to look out of a window. I'd always tried to show Mother love and respect, but sometimes my real feelings spilled out. "*Now* it's your charities," I said. "When I was a child, it was *'the theater.'*" I knew I wasn't showing up to very good advantage in front of Dan, but I'd had about all I could take from everybody.

Again Mother said, "Oh, don't be tiresome. Shall we sit down? When Mary gets back, she'll fix us some tea or, if you'd prefer, cocktails."

Dan waited for us to be seated; then he sat down on a green tapestry chair opposite where Mother and I were sitting on a period sofa. I could tell he was trying not to stare at Mother, but he was very much interested in her. She really was an attractive woman: tall, stately and slender — Park Avenue perfection. She wore her slightly blued gray hair fixed in a smooth roll around her head; rather old-fashioned, but becoming to her. Her faded blue eyes were always framed by lashes which she darkened, and she put a blue shadow on her lids and a very faint touch of rouge on her cheeks. She used a light-colored lipstick.

That day she was wearing a gray wool dress that I knew she'd paid a lot for. Its very simplicity showed it was expensive. And on one shoulder she wore a silver pin set with amethyst. The pin had belonged to her mother.

She asked Dan, "Are you still staying with Amelia?"

He said, "Yes, for the present."

Mother glanced at me. "How does Bryan like that?"

I couldn't help smiling. "I really don't know. Nor do I care."

Mother settled a small pillow behind her back. "Bryan has been very nice to you," she said. "I should think you would consider his feelings."

I tried not to show my annoyance. "Bryan has been very nice to me — up to a point. Beyond that he has made himself somewhat objectionable."

"You mean he has made love to you?"

"That — and other things."

"What do you mean by other things?"

I sighed. I realized this wasn't a very nice way to entertain Dan, but Mother always seemed to back me into a corner so I felt I had to fight back. I said, "Well, he tried to get me to invest what money I have the way he wanted me to. I've been doing all right the way things are. As a matter of fact, I've asked him for a complete accounting of all my investments. I've been thinking of turning over my business to my bank, or back to Mr. Wells." I hadn't told Dan this, and I saw him raise an eyebrow.

Mother said, "I suppose Jack left a will? You're so close-mouthed you never tell me anything."

I guess my lips tightened. I knew Dan was watching me. I said, "Yes, Jack left a will. He left everything to me."

Mother brightened at that and moved closer to me on the sofa. "Then you should be a very rich woman."

I said, "Yes, I suppose so."

Mother never let well enough alone. She

said, "I thought you liked Bryan. After all, he *is* your lawyer. He is supposed to give you advice. Are you intimating you don't trust him any more?"

"Not exactly. We just don't see eye to eye about — well, a lot of things."

Mother could never realize when she'd gone too far. She persisted, "When did you change your mind about him?"

I shrugged, gritting my teeth. "I don't know, exactly."

"You used to like him."

"Yes, I did, even though Jack didn't."

Mother turned to Dan. "Have you met Bryan?"

He said, "Yes, I have. He seems very capable."

"*That* he is," I agreed. "Capable, a pleasant companion for an evening when he wants to be. But that's all."

"You could do worse — for a second husband," Mother told me tartly.

It was a tactless remark, and I could feel my face flushing. "At the moment," I said, "I am not considering a second husband." I could feel the tears welling up, and my voice sounded choked as I added, "And if ever I do, it won't be Bryan Hancock!"

Fortunately, just then Mary and Ronny came in, and for the next hour there was the confusion of tea being served and Ronny spilling a glass of milk. When Dan and I got up to leave, Ronny cried at being left with his grandmother.

I soothed him as best I could and promised his grandmother would bring him home for a visit some day later in the week. With Mary's help, Dan and I managed to get away.

I was near tears and exhausted by the time we got into a taxi and started back home. It was a wrench for me to leave Ronny, but I felt he was safer with Mother at the present time. Dan, sensing my feelings, took my hand and squeezed it. I moved closer to him and laid my aching head against his broad shoulder. "I don't know what I'd do without you," I told him in a shaky voice. "You're very nice."

He put an arm around me and held me close. In my ear he whispered, "You're rather nice yourself. I've never felt so close to anyone before."

But when we reached the house, our closeness was shattered. Bryan was waiting for us. He was pacing up and down the dropped living room, and the ash tray on the coffee table was full of half smoked cigarettes. "Oh, there you are!" he said as we came in. "Where have you been?"

I slipped out of my coat and hung it on the newel post of the banister. "Up to Mother's," I told him.

"With this man?" He glared at Dan.

I went down the two steps to the living room and sank down on one end of the sofa. "Yes," I said. "And for heaven's sake, sit down and stop pacing back and forth like a caged lion."

Poor Dan! He'd been in the middle of an argument up at Mother's, and now here he was in the middle of an altercation between Bryan and me. Standing at the top of the two steps, he said, "If you'll excuse me, I'll go up to my room."

"Yes, do!" Bryan snapped rudely.

I said, "No, don't, Dan. I'd like you to stay." Then to Bryan I said, "I'll give the orders in my home, if you don't mind, Bryan."

He scowled at me. "Amelia, you're a fool!"

I smiled slightly. "Thanks," I said. "Now I finally know what you think of me."

He came and sat down beside me. "You know very well what I think of you," he said tensely. "I just don't want anything to happen to you."

I couldn't argue with that, so I turned and smiled at Dan. "Come and sit down, Dan," I said. "I'd like you and Bryan to get better acquainted."

He shrugged, came down the two steps and went over and sat down in the cherry brocade chair. I said to Bryan, "Dan has been kind enough to stay here with me, and I appreciate it. I wouldn't want to be here without a man to look after me."

Bryan's lips tightened. "You know I'd be glad to stay here with you. And you'd be safe with me."

I couldn't help smiling. "Would I? I'm not so sure."

Anger came into his eyes. "What do you mean by that?"

Dan moved uneasily in his chair. Breaking into the conversation, he said, "Perhaps I could persuade you both to have dinner with me? I passed a nice-looking French restaurant the other day down in the Fifties near Park Avenue."

I smiled at him gratefully. "I think that would be very nice. Don't you, Bryan?"

For a moment Bryan looked like a gathering thundercloud, so I put a hand on his arm. "Please, Bryan," I said. "For me?"

I knew my touch would melt him and felt somewhat ashamed of myself for taking advantage of his feeling for me. After a moment's hesitation, he patted my hand. "All right," he said grudgingly. "For you. But —" he stiffened defensively — "it will be as *my* guests."

Dan opened his mouth to protest, but I beat him to it. "That's being ungracious," I told Bryan gently. "Dan has invited us. Next time we will be your guests."

I could see the thought behind his cold blue eyes. "There won't *be* any *next* time — with *him.*" But all he said was, "Very well."

I stood up. "Suppose you men have a drink while I make a quick change?" I suggested. "Or do you want to freshen up, too?" I asked Dan.

Gratefully, I thought, Dan grabbed at my suggestion. Quickly he said, "I *would* like a shower and a change of clothes, if Bryan will excuse me?"

"Sure, go ahead," Bryan said surlily. And Dan and I went upstairs together.

Chapter Ten

Afterward, I couldn't honestly say our evening was a success. On the other hand, maybe it was. At least Dan learned more about Bryan.

I had done my best to dress in something I knew was becoming. I'd selected a black dress, but not mourning. It was cut simply but exquisitely and fitted my rather full figure without a wrinkle. It was floor-length with a simple shirtwaist-type bodice. I brushed my auburn hair up into a pile of curls on top of my head and wore only one piece of jewelry: a diamond and pearl pin on my left shoulder. I wore a waist-length blond mink cape and black high-heeled sandals.

The restaurant Dan had selected was one of those exclusive places with banquette seats at each side and just a few tables in the middle of the room. The waiters were attentive and the food excellent.

At first, making conversation with Bryan was difficult. But after two double dry martinis, to Dan's and my one apiece, he did most of the talking himself, addressing his remarks to me and ignoring Dan as much as possible. His main topic was money and investments. He said to me, "I wish you'd take my advice about buying that railroad stock. It's low now, but it's going to go up in a couple of months."

"That little railroad out west somewhere?" I asked, having listened to him praise its potentialities so many times I was tired of it. "And sell my AT&T and my General Motors to do it?"

"Why not?" he asked. "I've invested a good portion of my own money in it. They're going to merge with one of the big roads, and that will send the stock zooming up."

I shrugged. "That's what you hope. And it's your privilege to invest your money in whatever you want. But I prefer to leave my investments just as they are."

"Don't you trust my judgment?" His lips twisted into a sneer, and I was sorry Dan had to see that expression on his face.

I patted his hand, which was resting on the table with a half smoked cigarette between his fingers. "I trust your judgment as a lawyer, but not as a banker. And I wish you'd hurry up and give me an accounting of my investments."

His lips tightened. "The list is almost

ready," he said. "My secretary was working on it this morning. But I don't like your attitude at all, Amelia. You act as if you thought I was a crook." He pulled his hand away from mine with an annoyed gesture. "Is it because I lost money on the do-it-yourself company last month?"

I glanced over at Dan apologetically. "This must be boring for Dan," I said. "Suppose we change the subject?"

Coming to my rescue, Dan suggested, "Why don't we go see a play? Do you think we could get tickets this late?"

"Probably to something, but not to any of the popular plays."

Bryan scrunched out his cigarette in his coffee cup. "I don't want to see a play," he said petulantly.

I gathered my wrap around me, with Dan's help. "Then let's go home," I said.

Dan motioned to the waiter, got the check, and we stood up to leave.

Bryan put an arm around my waist to maneuver me closer to him and away from Dan.

In the taxi, I suggested we drop Bryan off at his apartment first, to which he objected. But I gave the driver his address and we all settled back in the seat, I in the middle. Bryan tried to hold my hand, but I managed to avoid him. And when the taxi stopped in front of his apartment, he leaned over and kissed me, then got out reluctantly, saying, "I'll call you tomorrow."

Dan said, "Good night, Bryan," but he merely nodded. At least he was honest enough not to lie and say he had enjoyed the evening.

When Dan and I were alone in the taxi, I moved closer to him and slipped my arm around his. "It was very nice of you to entertain Bryan and me," I told him, "and I'm very ashamed of the way Bryan acted."

He took hold of my hand, which was resting on his forearm, and squeezed it. "He isn't your responsibility."

"He's my friend, and you've been through enough unpleasantness because of me."

He smiled. "Don't worry about it."

The taxi was stopping before my house, and Dan paid the driver and helped me out. As we entered the house, Boy ran downstairs to meet us, barking with pleasure. I said, "Ssshhh!" and patted his head to quiet him. Then I asked Dan, "Would you like a cup of coffee or something?"

He said, "No, thank you," and we put out the downstairs lights and went up to our respective rooms, Boy loping up the stairs ahead of us. As we were going up, we could hear Althea snoring. I suppose she was so used to Boy barking she didn't even hear him any more.

In the second floor hallway, I turned to Dan and said, "Good night. It was a nice evening." For a moment we stood looking at each other in the shaded hall light. I was aching to have him put his arms around me and kiss me, and from the look in his eyes I was sure that was what he wanted to do. But he hesitated, and the moment passed. He merely patted my shoulder and said, "Good night."

Chapter Eleven

As the days passed, Inspector Keen kept reminding me he was still working on our case, and at least once a day he would ask some more questions and make veiled threats. He made me into a nervous wreck, and I could tell that Dan didn't feel too secure either. I presume that was Keen's way of trying to break us down so we'd tell the truth — or the truth as he would like it to be so he could wind up the case. I always had the feeling I was being watched, and I didn't like it.

One day he said, "We've been checking on that Sylvia. She was married to Nikki Radzinski before she married Evers."

Dan said, "Oh? Does that tighten the screws on Nikki ?"

Keen said, "Not yet. She had been divorced even before she married Nikki."

"A *femme fatale*," Dan quipped.

"More of a little gold digger," Keen said. "She was also a junkie. Picked it up down in South America."

"I wonder if Jack knew that?" I asked.

He shrugged. "Sometimes they can keep it covered up. At first anyway."

Dan's vacation was over, and he was going down to the office every morning. His boss had decided he'd better stay in town until everything was straightened out. Or perhaps Inspector Keen had suggested to J.C. that that would be best.

Whenever I caught sight of myself in a mirror, I realized I looked more and more as if the slightest breath of air would knock me over. I'd lost quite a lot of weight in a short time. Dan kept at me to see a doctor, but I insisted I was all right.

Nikki had become a permanent part of our ménage, coming every morning but Sunday and staying most of the day. He had a way with him that won over even Althea. He made his *coup d'état* with her when he taught her to make Hungarian goulash the way his grandmother used to make it. And he used to tease her and make her laugh until her entire body shook with reflex merriment.

He told me stories about Hungary and about his trip through middle Europe with a vaudeville troupe, and he painted word pictures of the small towns in the Balkans that made me want to take the first plane over and see them for myself.

He had even gained Dan's confidence, so that when Dan went to work each morning he'd stopped cautioning me to, "Take care and watch Nikki."

I was always able to find something for Nikki to do, and he was very handy at fixing things, taking Boy out for his walks and even entertaining Aunt Edna. He seemed able to handle her without upsetting her, and for that, I was very grateful to him.

But all that made it more complicated. *Somebody* must have stuck that knife in Dan's hat, with the threatening note speared to the blade. Also, *somebody* must have taken the trouble to put the phosphorus in the bread from which those sandwiches were made. But who? Phosphorus was what one might call an old-fashioned way to poison anyone. Nowadays there were all kinds of new drugs accessible to too many people with vicious intentions. So why choose phosphorus? It must have been somebody who was very naive.

On the face of it, it seemed as if it must have been somebody in the house. Of course Althea could have done it, but I couldn't believe that. And I knew it couldn't have been Aunt Edna, because she never went down in the kitchen. And of course I knew I hadn't done it. But I was the only one who knew I hadn't. Inspector Keen didn't know for sure, and neither did Dan, although I was certain Dan didn't suspect me.

Then one night Dan woke up with the feeling that something was wrong. He told me about it afterward, because at the time I was out of the running, so to speak. He said he lay perfectly still, listening. There wasn't a sound. He couldn't even hear Althea snoring. Then a board creaked in the hall, and instantly he was on his feet and out the door. In the hall, he bumped into something. There was the feel of cold steel along the side of his neck.

Instinctively he remembered a jujitsu trick he'd learned once, and grabbed for the back of his assailant's neck. But just then whoever was attacking him let out a piercing scream. Dan laughed a little and said, "I must admit it frightened me, and my hold was weakened."

Then Boy, who was in my room, began to bark furiously. I woke up and snapped on a light which shone into the hall, and Dan was able to see, to his dismay, that he was trying to throw Althea. She was in a voluminous pink and white-striped flannel nightdress, and she had a pair of shiny, long, slender and very sharp-pointed scissors in her hand.

I sat up in bed and called, "What's wrong?"

Dan glared at Althea. "That's what I'd

152

like to know, too," he said. "I heard a noise, and I found Althea prowling along the hall with —" he took the scissors away from her and brandished them so I could see them — "with these vicious-looking things," he added.

Althea began to sniffle. "You just about scared me to death!" she accused him. "And you hurt my neck." She began to rub the back of her neck and to twist her head to see if she could move it.

I asked, "What were you doing in the hall, Althea?"

"I was going to the bathroom," she told me. "And I wanted to protect myself in case I met somebody that shouldn't be here. I'm going to protect myself whenever I can."

I pulled the bedcovers up to my chin. I was wearing a sheer lacy nightdress that didn't give me much protection, either visually or thermally. "Well," I said, "you don't have to protect yourself by scaring everybody else. Now you've got me imagining I've been hearing things, I haven't slept much since I went to bed."

Dan asked, "Do you want me to go downstairs and see if everything is all right?" He had on his pajamas and bathrobe, and his hair was practically standing on end. He looked very manly.

I reached for a pale blue quilted robe, slipped it on and got out of bed. "I'll go with you," I told him as I stuck my cold feet into blue satin mules. "Althea, you go back to bed."

Althea shuffled into her room and slammed the door, and I said to Dan, "Perhaps we'd better take Boy with us."

At the sound of his name, Boy came out of my room and went downstairs with us, his heavy footsteps making more noise than mine or Dan's, especially as Dan was in his bare feet.

We turned on all the lights on the first floor and the basement, but everything was all right. The doors and windows were all locked, and there was no sign of an intruder.

Satisfied that nothing was wrong, we put out the lights and went back upstairs. As we reached the second floor, Dan said, "I think I'll go upstairs and have a look around. Just a minute until I get my slippers." He went into his room and returned with a pair of brown leather slippers on his feet, which by that time must have been good and cold.

Boy and I followed him up the stairs. But everything was all right up there, too. Aunt Edna's room was untouched, and the skylight was closed and hooked. I said, "Well, let's go back to bed. I guess everything is all right." I put out the lights, and Dan and Boy followed me down to the second floor. At my door Dan asked, "Can't you take something to help you sleep?"

I shook my head. He gently touched my cheek with a cold hand, and Boy and I went into my room. Aunt Edna was sleeping peacefully. That was one helpful thing about her: she always slept well.

The next day was Saturday, and Dan didn't have to go to his office. Nikki arrived early to do the Venetian blinds in the dropped living room and the back sitting room. They were so big it was quite a project to clean them, and it was too much for Althea.

Since Nikki had been working around the place and taking him for walks, he'd made friends with Boy, who by now followed him around like a shadow. Nikki would talk to him as if he were a person, and the dog would cock his head to one side and listen as if he really understood what was being said to him. Occasionally Nikki would have one of his headaches and have to sit down for a while, and Boy would go and sit very close to him and lick his cheek and his hands to show he was sympathetic. It was rather touching.

Ronny, too, seemed to be Nikki's slave

whenever they were together. That Saturday afternoon, Mother brought him down to see me. But after a while Mother said she wanted to go upstairs and see Aunt Edna. So I went into the sitting room, where Dan was reading a newspaper. I had some mending to do, so I sat down near him. He looked over his paper at me and smiled a welcome. I smiled back and felt a nice tingling sensation creep through me. I had to admit it was nice having him around. He was the kind of a man you could be comfortable with without talking all the time. Ronny came in and looked around for something to do. And then, just as I was about to give him a pencil and some paper from the desk so he could draw pictures, which he loved to do, Dan reached into a side pocket of his sports jacket and produced a baseball.

"For me?" Ronny asked, his eyes shining with pleasure.

"All for you," Dan told him.

"Will you play with me?" Ronny asked eagerly.

"Some day," Dan promised. "But we can't play in the house. We might break something."

"Can I show it to Nikki?" Ronny asked.

"Sure," Dan said. I couldn't help thinking

that the children-and-dogs theory was being smashed to bits, or else it was right and Nikki was really okay — a good guy.

Ronny ran down into the living room. Nikki was on a tall ladder, washing the top of a blind. "Look, Nikki," Ronny cried. "Look what Uncle Dan just gave me."

Nikki said, "A baseball. And a real one. Do you know how to play?"

"No, but Uncle Dan promised to play with me sometime. Do you know how to play?"

"Sure. I can do anything."

"You can? I thought you were just the grocery boy."

"Oh no. That was just make-believe."

"Then you weren't really the grocery boy?"

"No."

"Then what *are* you?"

Nikki smiled; he had a very nice smile. "Well, I'll tell you," he said. "You've seen that big bright star that seems to outshine all the others?" He came down the ladder and sat on a lower step so his head would be on a level with Ronny's.

"I guess so," Ronny said. "I don't get to see stars much. I always have to go to bed."

Dan and I exchanged sympathetic glances. Adults don't always realize what they do to children.

Nikki said, "Well, that big bright shiny star is named Mars. Now on Mars there are a lot of supermen, and once in a long, long while, one of them decides to do the earth a favor by visiting it, for what you people down here call a lifetime."

"I saw pictures of Mars on TV once, but it wasn't all bright and shiny, and there weren't any supermen in the pictures."

Dan winked at me, and I couldn't help smiling.

Nikki said, "You didn't see the other side of Mars. The supermen are on the other side."

Ronny's eyes opened wide. "Oh!" he said. "Are you really a superman?"

"Of course I'm a superman." Then in a stage whisper he added, "But don't tell anybody, because just ordinary folks would laugh. Only somebody smart, like you, would know it's true."

Ronny's admiration was exceeded only by Boy's devotion to the unknown quantity in our midst called Nikki. Now Ronny's childish face was alight with interest and excitement. "I won't tell a single person," he promised solemnly. "Except I'd like to tell Mommy."

Nikki said, "Well, I guess that will be all right. Mommies are different."

Dan got up and sauntered down into the living room. "Hi, Nikki," he said. "You seem to have a way with children and dogs."

Nikki shrugged. "I like children and dogs. They're not mixed up, like people."

Just then Mother came downstairs, calling, "Come on, Ronny. It's time for us to go."

Ronny began to wail, so I decided I'd better get into the act. I put down my mending and went down into the living room. "Must you go so soon?" I asked Mother. "Won't you wait and have some tea?"

Mother stood at the top of the two steps near the front door. "No, thank you. Come, Ronny!"

Ronny said, "No, I don't want to. I want to stay home." He moved nearer Nikki for protection.

Mother said, "Ronny, obey me!"

But Ronny only shrank nearer to Nikki, who put an arm around him.

I said, "Please, Mother, he's only a child. And no child is an angel."

Mother sniffed and began putting on her gloves. "Ronny is completely spoiled," she told me. "But if I have him a little while longer, I'll have him trained. And," she added, "the way you spend money on Edna is perfectly ridiculous! She doesn't need all those clothes. A couple of cheap house-dresses would do her perfectly well."

I chewed at my lower lip a moment before saying, "Aunt Edna is *my* responsibility. *You* didn't want to be bothered with her, yet you refuse to let me put her into a sanitarium where she would receive scientific care. So suppose you let me take care of her in my own way." I didn't like having to speak to Mother like that in front of Nikki and Dan, but she had a way of goading me into getting annoyed with her.

She sniffed. "Come, Ronny. We're going now. And I mean *now.*" She had his hat and coat under her arm and held them out to him.

Reluctantly he went to her, and she put the things on him, none too gently, snatching the baseball and throwing it down into the living room.

Ronny looked at me with tears in his eyes. "Mommy, I don't want to go with her! Can't I stay home?" he wailed.

I looked at Dan. He said, "Things aren't settled yet." And of course I knew what he meant. So I went over to Ronny, leaned down and hugged him and kissed his fore-head. "Be a good boy now," I told him. "And say goodbye to Uncle Dan and Nikki.

And be a brave boy. Some day soon, you'll be able to come home."

Tears began to run down his cheeks, and he stuck out his little chin and said, "Goodbye, Nikki."

Nikki said, "Goodbye, pal. And don't forget what I told you."

Ronny smiled through his tears. "I won't," he promised.

Dan said, "Goodbye, Ronny. See you soon."

He looked at Dan pleadingly, and Dan looked at me. But what could we do? It wouldn't be good for the child to be around when Inspector Keen was asking questions. And none of us felt too safe in the house, with the murders still unsolved. Seeing he wasn't going to get any help from either Dan or me, Ronny pulled in a quivering breath and said, "Bye, Uncle Dan. Thanks for the baseball."

"You're welcome," Dan told him. "Some day we'll have a game, you and I. And I'll take care of the ball for you."

His little face brightened at that, but Mother grabbed his shoulder. "Oh, come along!" she said impatiently, and pushed him out of the front door ahead of her.

Nikki returned to his cleaning of the Venetian blind, and Dan went back to his newspaper. Suddenly I wanted to be alone with Dan, even if we just sat near each other without talking. So as the front door slammed behind Mother and Ronny, I turned to Nikki. "Nikki, will you let that go now, and go up and wash the paint in my aunt's room? She seems quiet now, and you have a way with her. You seem to know just what to say." What I really meant, in addition to wanting to be alone with Dan, was that I was sure Mother had upset Aunt Edna, and maybe Nikki could talk to her and quiet her down. At the moment I didn't feel equal to it.

Nikki said, "Yes, ma'am," picked up his pail of water and rags and went upstairs.

I called after him. "If you need more cloths, you will find some in that closet in the third floor hall. And you can get fresh water in one of the bathrooms."

Nikki said, "Yes, ma'am," and disappeared up the stairs just as the front doorbell rang. I opened the door, and my heart sank. Bryan was standing there. Not too cordially I said, "Oh, hello, Bryan. Come in."

Bryan looked at me with such open admiration I was instantly ashamed of myself for not wanting to see him. I had on a green shirtwaist-type wool dress, and my hair was tied back in a pony tail with a green ribbon.

Bryan came into the hall and smiled down at me. "How are you today, my dear?" he asked.

I said, "Fine, thank you." He took off his overcoat and hat and put them on the chair by the hall railing. Then he glanced through to the sitting room and discovered Dan. Dan folded his newspaper and said, "Greetings, Hancock." It was the first time they'd met since our evening on the town.

Bryan glared at Dan. "You still here?" he asked. His tone was insolent, and I could see Dan resented it. I didn't blame him. Bryan went down into the living room, rubbing his hands as if they were cold. "Don't you think you've been hanging around here long enough?" he demanded.

Dan smiled at him; knowing how he must feel, I thought it was decent of him. He said, "When I do, I'll pack up and go. And as I remember it, we've been through this before."

I followed Bryan down into the living room. "Come now, boys; don't fight," I said with forced cheerfulness.

Just then there was a sound of furniture being moved upstairs. A woman screamed. Then there was silence.

Bryan, Dan and I looked at one another, each of us startled, frightened and apprehensive. Then Bryan asked, "What was that?"

With what voice I could command, I said, "I can't imagine."

Dan brushed past both of us and started up the front stairs. But just then Nikki came down the stairs, carrying Aunt Edna, who seemed to be unconscious.

With my heart hammering and my stomach quavering, I helped Nikki lay Aunt Edna on the sofa in the living room. "What happened?" I asked Nikki, my voice shaking.

Nikki, looking terrified, said, "I don't know for sure. I was shoving that big highboy across the room so I could get at the woodwork behind it when I accidentally hit that fancy chandelier with it, and it tore loose from the ceiling. It didn't fall, but it swung around like crazy, and the old dame screamed and fell in a heap. I thought I'd better bring her down here, in case the thing really did crash down."

I dropped on my knees beside the sofa and rubbed one of Aunt Edna's limp hands. "It must have shocked her," I explained, "seeing the chandelier. Years ago she saw her brother-in-law, my father, killed by a similar chandelier falling on him, in a show they were in. That was what made her sick."

Nikki was standing beside me, looking down at Aunt Edna with honest concern in his dark eyes. "Yes," he said, "I guess that chandelier could kill a person. But it didn't fall down. It just tore loose." He looked at me pleadingly. "I'm sorry," he said. "I should have watched where I was pushing that highboy."

"It's all right, Nikki," I told him. "You didn't mean to do it."

Dan asked, "Hadn't we better call the doctor? It's probably just shock, but even so —"

I started to get to my feet, and Dan and Nikki helped me. "Yes," I said, "I'll call him right away." I hurried into the back room to use the phone.

Bryan, who had been standing to one side and doing nothing to help, suddenly came to life. Officiously he announced, "Guess I'll go upstairs and have a look around."

Neither Nikki nor Dan answered him, and he stalked out of the room and up the stairs with more officiousness than Inspector Keen himself would have shown.

Nikki lit a cigarette with hands that were trembling. I heard him say, "Tell me about the old dame. Does she ever make sense?"

Dan said, "I don't know. I've only seen her a few times, even though I've been living here. She is very quiet."

Nikki sank down on a nearby chair as if he no longer trusted his legs to hold him up and ran a hand over the top of his head, holding it there for a moment. Then, muttering to himself, he said, "That damn head of mine!" He looked up at Dan. "When I first went upstairs just now, she was in a stew about some queer-looking matches."

As I talked on the phone, Dan and I exchanged quick glances. Then nonchalantly Dan said, "Oh, the lucifer matches? I understand she prizes them very highly. I believe she thinks some of them are missing. She probably had them counted. She claims she gave some of them to someone one night, and she regrets it."

I feared Dan was taking a long chance telling Nikki about the matches, and as I talked to our doctor, Doctor James, on the phone, I watched Nikki's reaction, as did Dan. But all Nikki said was, "They're queer-looking things."

"Yes, they are," Dan agreed. "As near as I can tell, they are about the first friction matches ever made. They're probably well over a hundred years old. They used to call them lucifer matches. The heads are made of white sulphur. It's very poisonous."

Nikki's face was perfectly blank for a moment; then suddenly a look of hatred came into his eyes. Then he looked down at the lighted end of his cigarette, and I couldn't see his eyes any more. After a moment he said, "Queer old dame."

I'd finished my call and joined them down in the living room. "Where's Bryan?" I asked.

Dan said, "He went up to have a look at Aunt Edna's room."

I said, "Oh," and went over to examine Aunt Edna, who was still unconscious. Then, looking up at Dan, I said, "Maybe I'd better send for Mother."

"She couldn't have reached home yet, could she?"

"No, I guess not. But Mary is there. She can tell Mother to come right back here as soon as she gets home."

"Want me to phone her?"

"Will you, please? You'll find the number in that little book on the desk. Gifford. Mrs. Ronald Gifford."

As Dan started for the back room, he asked, "What about Ronny?"

"Mary will take care of him."

Dan went into the back room, picked up the phone and ruffled through the little book in which I kept often used numbers. I knelt down beside Aunt Edna. Nikki said,

"If there isn't anything else I can do, is it all right if I go now? My head is starting to kick up."

I said, "Yes, Nikki. There won't be anything more today. And thank you for helping." I turned my attention to Aunt Edna and didn't notice what Nikki did.

Dan finished phoning and came into the living room. "The maid said she would tell your mother." Then he looked around and asked, "Did Nikki go back upstairs?"

I said, "I don't think so. I told him he could go home. His head was bothering him." As I was speaking, Bryan came down from the third floor. "Did Nikki go upstairs?" I asked him.

Bryan said, "I didn't see him. Maybe he went down to the kitchen."

Suddenly a feeling of apprehension swept through me. I'd been thinking Nikki was all right, but recollection of that look of hatred that had come into his eyes when he was talking to Dan made me begin to doubt him again. Sensing my apprehension, Dan said, "We should have watched him."

I didn't answer, and he went out into the hall and called, "Althea."

"Yes, sir," Althea called back. "You want something?"

"Is Nikki down there?"

"No, sir. He hasn't been down here since lunch."

Dan said, "All right," and came back into the living room. "He isn't downstairs," he told me.

I got to my feet. "Stop worrying," I said. "He probably went home. I'm sure he is all right."

"I hope so," he said.

Bryan had strolled over to a front window. Whirling around, he said, "Amelia, I wish you'd let me take charge here. This whole set-up is ridiculous!"

My nerves suddenly cracked, and I screamed, "Oh, shut up, Bryan! And go away! You get on my nerves!"

For a moment he looked as if I'd slapped his face. Then he stamped over and picked up his hat and coat. "Very well, if that is the way you feel about it!"

Bursting into tears, I covered my face with my hands. Bryan went out, slamming the door behind him. For a moment Dan just stood beside me. Then he took me into his arms, and suddenly I began to feel better. Just being held close to him made everything easier to bear.

Chapter Twelve

We were interrupted by the rearrival of my mother. When I opened the door for her, she sailed in with all the aplomb of the S.S. *Queen Elizabeth* entering New York Harbor. "*Now* what is the matter?" she demanded.

I said, "Aunt Edna," and led her down into the living room and over to the sofa where Aunt Edna lay, still unconscious.

"What's the matter with her?" Mother asked, showing no emotion but annoyance.

"Nikki was cleaning her room, and he inadvertently shoved that tall highboy into the light fixture. It tore loose and began swinging back and forth, just on the wires. It — well, it shocked her. Can't you understand? It shocked her into remembering, and she screamed and collapsed."

Mother stood beside her unconscious sister and looked down at her with cold, expressionless eyes. "So what do you expect *me* to do about it?" she asked.

Suddenly I began to feel limp. I couldn't help sighing. "Nothing, I guess, except — well, I thought you ought to know. After all, you *are* her sister."

Mother said, "Yes, so I am. Have you sent for the doctor?"

"Of course. At least give me credit for that much sense!"

Not wanting to interfere between us, Dan lit a cigarette and walked over to the front windows.

Then, all of a sudden, Mother began to cry. At first she made no sound; tears were just running down her face. Then she began to make strange noises in her throat. Finally she got hysterical, dropping to her knees beside her sister, kissing her unconscious face, sobbing endearing names and begging Edna to speak to her.

No one had heard Althea come up from the basement until she said sharply, "Elizabeth Julliard! You stop that!"

Mother stopped crying and looked up at Althea. For a moment she just stared at her as if she didn't recognize her.

Althea went to her and helped her to her feet. "You did that scene just swell in *The Lady Repents*, but that was a long time ago."

Mother caught her breath; then she cried, "Oh, Althea!" and threw herself into Althea's ample arms.

For several minutes Althea let her cry quietly on her shoulder. Then, patting her back gently, she said, "There, there, honey. Stop crying now. Althea understands. But crying won't make things better."

The doorbell rang. I said, "That's probably Doctor James," and went to open the door.

It was the doctor, and I gave him a quick briefing in the hall. After he went into the living room and had examined Aunt Edna, he said, "I'd suggest we get her up to Eastview Sanitarium just above White Plains. I'll make arrangements for a private ambulance."

There was nothing I could do but acquiesce, so I nodded mutely and waited while he went into the sitting room and did the necessary phoning.

Althea had gotten Mother to sit down in a chair and brought her a glass of water. When Doctor James finished on the phone, he came and got some pills from his bag and gave Mother two of them. "Here, take these, Mrs. Gifford," he said. "They will calm your nerves."

Mother took them, put them into her mouth and drank some water. "Isn't it awful?" she said.

Dr. James shrugged. "It may be for the best," he told her. Then he came over to me. "How about you?" he asked. "Do you feel the need of something?"

I shook my head. "No, I'm all right."

Mother waited until Aunt Edna had been taken away; when she decided to go home, Dan went out with her and put her into a taxi.

After Mother had gone, Althea said, "I'll make a pot of tea," and shuffled off downstairs.

When Dan came in, he and I sat on the sofa, and it seemed the natural thing for him to put his arms around me. With a sigh I leaned my head against his shoulder. After a few moments of companionable silence, Dan asked, "What did Althea mean by what she said to your mother?"

"Well, Mother is apt to re-enact parts she has played, if she thinks they will fit the time and the place. Sometimes she gets away with it, and people think she is clever or witty or, extremely emotional — if they have never seen her in the particular play in which the scene was originally. That one was, as Althea said, from a show she did called, *The Lady Repents*. I recognized it but decided I wouldn't say anything. Besides, she wouldn't have paid any attention to me. Althea could always manage her. She's always let Althea boss her around. But Althea has been very good to her, too. Althea has been good to all of us."

In a few minutes Althea came upstairs with a tray holding a pot of tea, cups and saucers and a plate of small iced cookies. Dan and I pulled away from each other when we heard her coming.

"Thank you, Althea," I said, and began to pour the tea. Just then the phone rang.

Althea said, "Sit still. I'll answer it." She went into the sitting room and picked up the phone. "Evers' residence," she said, and I couldn't help smiling.

Then she said, "What is it, honey? Talk slower. I can't understand you."

I called, "Who is it?" and she told me, "Your mother."

"What does she want?"

Althea listened for a few minutes, shaking her head and saying, "Honey, calm down. Hysterics won't do any good. Didn't those pills the doctor gave you help?"

I got up from the sofa and went and took the phone from Althea. "What is it, Mother?" I asked.

"It's Ronny!" Mother screamed. "He's gone! Kidnaped!"

I sat down on the edge of the desk, afraid I was going to faint. Dan got up from the sofa, came back to the sitting room and whispered to Althea, "What is it?"

There was fright in Althea's dark eyes. "Something about little Ronny," she told him.

I was so limp by that time I could scarcely sit upright, and Dan just caught me as I sagged. Holding me with one arm, he picked up the phone, which I'd dropped on the desk, with his free hand and said into it, "Mrs. Gifford, this is Dan Brewster. Can you tell me what the matter is?"

"Oh, God!" I could hear my mother scream. "What's the matter with you all down there? Can't anyone understand English? Ronny is missing. Ronny! Ronny! Ronny! He's missing! Gone! Kidnaped!"

"But how? When?" Dan asked, and I could feel his whole body stiffen as I leaned against him.

"How? We don't know," my mother yelled into the phone. "Mary was in the kitchen, and Ronny was in my room watching television. But when Mary went in to see what he was doing, he was gone!"

"Gone? But where could he go?" Dan asked.

"How do I know?" Mother yelled. "Stop asking stupid questions! The window to the fire escape was open, but there isn't any sign of him out there. Can't you do something? You're a man, aren't you?"

"So I've been told."

"Oh, for heaven's sakes, don't get facetious!"

"I'm sorry," Dan said. "I suppose you've searched the apartment?"

"Of course."

"And the building?"

"Where would he be in the building if not here in the apartment?"

"A small boy could be almost anywhere, if he took it into his head to wander."

"Ronny never wanders when he's with me. He knows better."

Althea was helping Dan hold me so I wouldn't slip to the floor. I was beginning to wish Dan would stop talking to Mother so they could get me to the sofa. I felt so weak.

Evidently Dan had the same idea, because he said into the phone, "Well, you and Mary keep looking for him, and I'll call the police. I'll be in touch with you. And, Mrs. Gifford, don't worry. We'll find him."

I could hear the phone receiver bang, and Dan replaced the one he was holding. Then he and Althea helped me into the living room and onto the sofa. Dan slipped an arm under my head and managed to get some of the now lukewarm tea into my mouth, and Althea stood beside me, muttering, "Poor lamb. Poor lamb."

Gradually I could feel my strength

coming back. When I gave a sigh and said, "Thank you; I'm all right now," Dan turned me over to Althea and went back to the phone and called Inspector Keen. "It's the kid," he explained. "He's disappeared from his grandmother's."

Then he said, "We don't know whether he's just run away or been kidnaped."

Inspector Keen said something, and Dan responded, "We'd appreciate it. The quicker the better." He gave him Mother's address. Then he asked, "You remember what the child looks like?" Then, "Yes, that's right. Red hair. He's about four years old; blue eyes, nice-looking."

Inspector Keen asked him a question, and Dan turned to me. "Can you describe what he had on?"

I said, "Well, I presume he still had on what he wore down here: blue corduroy pants and a blue and white stripped T-shirt, with a navy coat sweater over it. He probably didn't have on his outdoor things."

Dan gave the description and said, "Let us know. And thanks, Inspector." He replaced the phone and came down into the living room. "Inspector Keen says not to worry. They'll have Ronny back before very long."

Chapter Thirteen

There must have been a newspaper reporter snooping around when Aunt Edna was taken out earlier, because that evening, the late editions of the tabloids had a picture of her being taken to the ambulance and even knew which sanitarium she'd been taken to.

That night, or rather about four o'clock in the morning, something awakened me. I'd taken a sleeping pill or I wouldn't have slept at all, so I was feeling kind of hazy.

Even before I opened my eyes, I felt a menacing presence near me. When I opened my eyes, the room was dark, but I could see an even darker form close to the bed. And I could hear breathing. There was a sweet, sickish odor in the room. I was too terrified to move. Then, as my eyes became accustomed to the dark, I was able to see a knife blade being held over me. Then it began coming down — slowly, then faster and faster, like lightning. It seemed like an eternity that I was too frightened to move. But it must have been only a fraction of a second, because just before the point of the knife touched me, I made an almost superhuman effort and rolled over to the other side of the bed and onto the floor between the beds, just as the knife struck. I heard it go into the mattress, slitting it, as it would have gone into my heart if I'd been on that spot.

Then the dark form leaped over the bed and grabbed me, and I fought with it desperately. It was probably only a few split-seconds, but it seemed like an eternity, before I was able to scream. Then strong, relentless fingers went around my throat. I must have blacked out, because the next thing I knew, I felt something pressing down on my back. I murmured, "Please, don't!" Then I heard myself moan. I managed to turn over on my side and felt of my throat, which seemed to hurt. Then I looked up and saw it was Dan standing over me. I managed to ask, "Why did you do it?"

He looked down at me, where I lay on the bed Aunt Edna had used. "You don't think I tried to choke you, do you?" he asked.

I didn't know what to think, and I guess my bewilderment showed. I glanced around the room, which was light enough now, because the door to the hall was open. Then I saw a knife sticking upright in *my* bed, the way the other knife had been sticking in Jack's back.

Laboriously I raised myself up on one

elbow and stared at the knife handle.

Althea had come from her room and was standing in the doorway with her bedclothes wrapped around her. Her face was a greenish gray, and her eyes bulged and rolled.

Dan sat down on the bed beside me and pulled a blanket over me because there was a cold wind blowing in from the hall and I didn't have anything on but a thin nightdress. "Could you see who your assailant was?" Dan asked. "Whoever it was was gone by the time I got here after you screamed."

Being suspicious that it might have been he, I could hardly look at him as I said, "No. But why were you poking me in the back?"

"I was giving you artificial respiration. You're sure your assailant was a *man?*"

"Yes — yes, I'm sure."

The phone rang, and we all looked at each other. There was an extension on the night table between the twin beds, but as I reached for it, Dan said, "Better let me answer it from downstairs."

I knew what we were all thinking. Had Ronny been found? And if he hadn't or had been found injured, Dan didn't want me to learn it over the phone that way. So he repeated, "I'll go downstairs." I could tell he didn't want to, but he would have done anything to save me from a shock. Then why did I think he had been the dark form bending over me with a knife? I guess I was just confused.

He started for the door, stepping over something on the way. Althea closed her eyes and moaned, and I sat up to see what it was. When I saw it was Boy, prostrate, as if he were dead, I managed to get to my feet and stagger over to him. Kneeling down beside him, I stroked his head. "Poor Boy!" I said, and tears ran down my cheeks.

The phone kept ringing, and at the doorway Dan said, over his shoulder, "He was chloroformed, but I think he'll be all right. Open the windows so he'll get air." Then he pushed past Althea and went downstairs.

Maybe I shouldn't have, but I couldn't resist picking up the phone on the night table and listening. A man's voice was asking, "Is this Mrs. Evers' residence?"

Dan said, "Yes."

"This is Doctor Enright at the Eastview Sanitarium. Is Edna Julliard there?"

I felt cold prickles creeping up my legs and going on a sepulcher-like walk up my spine. Dan said, "No. Why?"

"She's escaped. She's been gone for several hours. We can't find her anywhere.

181

We've called her sister, Mrs. Gifford, and she hasn't seen or heard from her."

Dan said, "Wait a minute," then I could hear him rushing around the first floor, opening and shutting the hall closet door, running down to the basement, then back up to the phone. He said, "I don't think she's here. But if you'll give me your number, I'll search the house and call you back."

The doctor gave his number. Then he said, "Perhaps you should know that Miss Julliard regained consciousness and became rational just a little while before she disappeared!"

I gasped, and Dan must have heard me, but he didn't let on. He just said, "Oh! Well, I'll call you back," and hung up the phone. So I dropped my receiver into place, too. But I could hear the clicking of Dan dialing a number, so I picked up my receiver again. He was saying, "Something queer is going on here, Sergeant. Perhaps you'd better send over a few men." Then he explained what had happened. When he finished his story, a man said, "Okay."

Then Dan asked, "Any word of the child?"

My stomach wobbled when I heard the man say, "Not yet."

"Have you searched Nikki's apartment?" Dan asked, to my surprise.

The man said, "Yes. The boy isn't there. Neither is Nikki."

Dan said, "Well, hurry those men, will you, please?"

"Right away."

The phone clicked off, and I dropped my receiver into place and hurried into my white quilted housecoat as Dan was coming up the stairs. Althea had gone into her room and returned in an electric blue quilted robe that made her look like a big blue tent. Her face had regained its normal color, but her eyes still looked frightened.

Coming into my room, Dan said, "I called the police."

Unashamedly I said, "I know. I listened."

"I was afraid of that," Dan said, shivering as a blast of wind blew down the stairs from the third floor. He pulled his robe more tightly around him. Then his, mine and Althea's eyes met, and all three of us looked anxiously up the stairs. The third floor was in darkness. Dan said, "Perhaps I'd better have a look up there."

I went out into the hall and snapped on a light switch that lighted up the third floor. Dan started up the stairs, and I followed. Before we reached the top, we saw the skylight was open. That was where the wind had been coming from.

I went into Aunt Edna's room and snapped on the lights. The room hadn't been touched since that afternoon. The highboy, covered with plaster, was still in the middle of the room. The crystal chandelier was hanging by the wires. The wind from the hall was swaying it back and forth gently. As it swung, the crystal prisms tinkled eerily.

I looked around the room, under the bed, in the closet, behind the window drapes, in the small bathroom. There was no one there.

As I made my search, Dan was close beside me. "Do you think Aunt Edna — ?" he asked.

I shivered, and not only because of the cold air coming down from the open skylight. "I don't know," I had to admit. "That doctor on the phone — he said she had become rational."

Dan said, "Yes." We went into the hall and looked up at the black rectangle, through which we could see a patch of starlit sky. "I'd better go up on the roof and have a look around."

But I threw my arms around him. "Oh, no!" I cried. "Please!"

He held me close, and I clung to him. He let his cheek rest against my hair for a moment. "But, darling," he said, "if there is anyone up there, I ought to find out and do something about it."

But I couldn't let him go. I was clinging to him so tightly I'm sure he could feel my heart pounding. "I won't let you go!" I said tensely. "If anything should happen to you, I'd die!" Then, startled at the vehemence of my words, I looked up at him. He bent his head and gently kissed my lips. "God bless you for saying that," he said. Then, gently but firmly putting me aside, he started up the ladder to the roof.

As I waited for him, I shivered from the icy wind. My lined, quilted robe felt like tissue paper, and I could imagine how cold Dan must be. His robe wasn't even lined. I went up a few steps of the ladder so I could watch him. He was looking behind the chimney and across the other roofs in both directions. Each house had a couple of chimneys, and he couldn't go prowling around looking behind every one of them. Besides, even if he tried, it would be very easy for someone to play hide and seek with him and never let Dan catch him. It was a dark night in spite of the stars, there was no moon, and the chimneys cast shadows even

185

darker than the night.

Dan came back to the skylight and began backing down the ladder, and I quickly got out of his way. "Nothing," he assured me, closing the skylight. He tried to hook it but discovered the hook had been pulled off.

I said, "Maybe we'd better go downstairs and wait for the police."

We went down to the second floor. Althea was waiting for us, trembling and panting as if she'd been running. I said, "Come on, Althea; we're going downstairs to wait for the police."

She moaned. "Lord have mercy on us! The police again!"

I said sharply, "Oh, hush, Althea!" So we trailed downstairs. In the dropped living room, I sank down on the sofa, and Dan lit cigarettes for us both and sank down beside me. Althea didn't smoke. I could feel Dan shivering from the cold. Althea sat on the edge of the cherry brocade wing chair on the other side of the coffee table. There was no fire in the fireplace, and the furnace had been turned low for the night, so the room was chilly.

Suddenly Dan said, "I'd better go up and see if I can do anything for Boy." But Althea said, "I worked with him while you were up on the roof. I got him so he's conscious. Poor beast!"

I realized that was probably why she had been so breathless. Bending over to work on a dog lying on the floor couldn't have been easy for anyone as heavy as she was. I said, "That was very nice of you, Althea. I should have remembered him myself."

"And so should I," Dan said.

For a while we sat without talking, but we were all doing a lot of thinking. Eventually I said, "I wish I knew where Ronny is."

Dan said, "The police will find him." He said it with far more confidence than showed in his face. Then he said, "Whoever attacked you, Amelia, chloroformed Boy, so it must have been someone he knew and trusted, or they wouldn't have been able to get close to him. Are you sure your assailant was a man?"

"Yes, I'm sure. I told you before." I shivered just thinking about it.

Althea said, "I wish the police would come. I don't like them, but it's kind of spooky here tonight. I never realized before what a big house this is."

I said, "Hush, Althea!" just as Nikki appeared at the top of the two steps down to the sitting room. He was breathing heavily, and I didn't like the look on his face.

Chapter Fourteen

I cried, "Nikki!"

He said, "Yes, it's me." He was pointing a gun at me, and Dan moved closer to me and put a protective arm around my waist. To Nikki he said, "What — no knives, Nikki?" I had the feeling Dan wasn't too surprised to see him.

Nikki came down the two steps and sauntered toward us. "I haven't got time for knives now," he said. "Bullets are quicker. Get away from the lady, Brewster."

Dan's arm around me tightened.

Nikki snapped, "Do as I tell you, or I'll plug the two of you together! As a matter of fact, get up on your feet, the two of you, and stand over there at the side of the room, in front of the railing."

Althea made a sound in her throat, and he said, "You too."

Dan still held onto me, but I pushed him away and got to my feet. "We'd better do as he says," I told Dan. I was surprised that my voice was calm and steady and my legs strong enough to take me over to the side of the room Nikki had indicated.

Muttering to herself, Althea got up and joined us. Dan said, "Don't be a fool, Nikki. The police will be here any minute. You'll be sure to get caught."

"That's why I've got to work fast!" Nikki took a better grip on his gun and aimed it at Dan. "I hate to eliminate you, Brewster," he said. "I've grown to sort of like you. But you're too smart and you know too much. When I get through, there isn't going to be anybody in this town who knows I'm mixed up with this Evers bunch. Keen's too dumb. Besides, after you and the beautiful redhead here, and my friend Althea —" He put his free hand up to his head as if he had one of his headaches. But he never took his eyes from us.

I could hear Althea gulp, but she didn't speak. Nikki went on, "Nobody will bother any more, after all you folks are gone. The police will get tired of the case and drop it. Anyway, I'll be in South America by to-morrow. I've got plane tickets, and I've got some money saved up. But first I want to tell you and Mrs. Evers a few things." He was talking directly to Dan.

I asked him, "Did you kill my husband, Nikki?"

He gave a quick glance. "No. Sylvia did."

"Sylvia?" My voice was charged with astonishment.

"That's right. Sylvia. Because she was going to have a baby, and he threatened to leave her and marry some other dame."

"How do you know?"

"She told me."

Dan gave me a questioning look, but I pretended not to see it.

Nikki answered the look, though, by saying, "Yes, she knew about the baby." He nodded toward me.

I asked, "But how do you know it was Sylvia who killed Mr. Evers?"

"Because that afternoon when I delivered the groceries — there was a big order, so I had to make two trips in from the truck — I left the basement door open after the first trip. And while I was getting the second box of stuff, I saw Sylvia dash down the steps of the areaway and go in the door."

"Well, what do you know!" Althea said.

"Shut up!" Nikki snapped at her.

Dan said, "So you followed her? Sylvia, I mean."

He said, "Yes. I didn't know what she was up to, so after I delivered the second box of stuff, I banged the door again and fixed the lock and the gate so I could get back in. Then I made another delivery around the corner, left the truck on the next block and came back. Althea didn't hear me. She had her radio going."

"Why, you sneaking — !" Althea exploded.

But he yelled, "Shut up!" at her. His voice was beginning to rise hysterically, but he lowered it as he began talking to me again. "I listened in the hall. Then I started tiptoeing up the stairs. But I heard you —" he nodded at Dan — "phoning the police, so I waited on the stairs. When you looked out in the hall, I was afraid you'd see me. But I flattened myself against the wall, and you didn't look down the stairs."

"My mistake," Dan said.

"When you came back into this room, I came up to find out if I could see anything."

"And could you?" Dan asked.

"Yes. I saw plenty! Jack Evers was on the floor, with one of my knives in his back."

"And you hadn't put it there?" Dan asked. It was a ridiculous conversation, but I could understand that Dan was keeping it going, hoping against hope that the police would arrive. Nikki's hand holding the gun was shaking now, but if Dan had made a dive for it, as I was sure he wanted to do, the thing could have gone off.

Nikki said, "I told you I didn't!" meaning put the knife in Jack's back. "But I took it out and took it with me. You were reading some letter, sitting here on the sofa," he told Dan.

Dan asked, "And where was Sylvia all this time?"

Althea and I were breathing so audibly they could hear us.

Nikki said, "She must have gone out while I was around the corner. So I decided I'd try to find her."

"And did you?" Dan asked.

"No, I didn't know where she and Evers were living any more, because she'd gotten scared of me and moved."

I could feel myself relaxing a little, and I think Dan was also. As long as Dan could keep Nikki talking, I felt we were safe. I was not a psychiatrist, but I could see he had reached the point where he had to tell the whole story. He'd lived with it alone for as long as he could.

Dan asked, "Just out of curiosity, how did you get out of here?"

Nikki drew in a deep breath and gripped the gun tighter in his trembling hand. "I got behind one of those long curtains in the back room. You had your back to me and didn't see me. Then, when all the fuss started out in the hall, I went out the back window, slid down the roof of that shed, went over the fence and got into that empty house next door."

"Then what did you do?" Dan prompted.

"Then I went up to the roof and across the roofs to the end of the block. The fire escapes of that apartment were close enough so I could jump to them. That way I got down to the yard and through the cellar and out to the street."

I started to sit down on a nearby chair, but Nikki yelled at me, "Stay where you are! It'll be easier to hit you if you're standing up!"

At that Dan made a lunge at him, but Nikki stuck the gun in his chest. I screamed, "Dan, don't!" got up from the chair and stood against the railing again. "Please, Dan, be careful," I said. "The police ought to be here soon."

Nikki's lips tightened over his white teeth in an ugly grimace. "That's right," he said. "We haven't got much time left. I'd better talk fast and shoot fast."

"Okay — talk," Dan said, backing away from him. "Then what?"

"So later I got to thinking about you, Brewster," he said. "I didn't know who you were, but I decided you might make a nuisance of yourself. So that evening I came back and got in through the skylight. It was a cinch to flip the hook with a penknife, and I wiped off all my fingerprints."

"Didn't Miss Julliard see you?" Dan asked. The conversation was getting a bit wearisome, and everybody's nerves were near the cracking point. But the longer Dan could keep Nikki talking, the nearer the police should be. They had promised to come right away, and it was at least an hour since Dan had called.

"Yes, she saw me," Nikki said, "and she asked me if I was Washington's aide. I could tell she was nuts, so I said, 'Sure.' Then we were pals, and she let me stay in the upper hall so I could listen to what was going on down here. After a while I heard you all go down to the basement. It seemed quiet then, so I tiptoed down. There wasn't anybody in sight, but I saw your hat and coat on that chair." He nodded at the one I had tried to sit on a few minutes before. "You were getting in my hair, so I wrote a warning note to you and stuck it on the knife I'd taken out of Evers' back."

I stifled a sob and shuddered.

Nikki noticed and glared at me. "Oh, it was clean," he explained. "I'd cleaned it off so there wouldn't be any blood or fingerprints on it."

I could tell Dan would have liked to make another lunge at him. But it was too dangerous. Instead he said, "And I suppose you got away over the roofs again?"

"That's right. But I came back again as soon as the cops got through looking. There wasn't anyone in this room, so I could get down the stairs without being seen. Sylvia and Mrs. Evers were in that back room, so I hid in the back of the hall and listened. I wanted to know what deviltry Sylvia was up to. I'd told her I was going to get even with the whole Evers family because Jack took her away from me. That's why I took the job with the grocery store where they traded, because that way I could get at them easy. But Sylvia got scared and was going to warn Mrs. Evers. She'd met me the day before and said she was going to tell, if I didn't get out of town." He was breathless after that long speech, and the hand holding the gun was trembling alarmingly.

"But you wouldn't go?" Dan encouraged him.

"I said I'd go if she'd go with me and we could have our act again."

"And she wouldn't?"

"She just laughed at me." There was so much bitterness in his voice I couldn't help feeling a little sorry for him.

I said, "It seems you and I have something in common, Nikki. We both lost the one we loved."

He said, "That's right. But it ain't going to save you now."

Still stalling for time, Dan requested, "Go on with your story, Nikki. Then what?"

"Well, Evers told Sylvia that morning — the morning of the day she killed him — that he was going to leave her. So she followed him here and let him have it. She had a case of my knives and thought she could pin it on me by using one of them."

"But they searched your room and didn't find anything."

"Yes, I know. The cops searched my room a couple of times. A friend of mine had all my knives that Sylvia didn't have. He was sharpening them for me. He has a store that does that."

Althea was beginning to whimper, and I said, "Ssshhh!" to her.

Dan asked Nikki, "Did you hear what Sylvia said to Mrs. Evers?" In an aside he said to me, "Sorry, dear, but this is necessary."

I said, "Yes, I understand."

Nikki said, "Yes, I heard. Mrs. Evers asked Sylvia, 'Did you know Jack was murdered here this afternoon'?"

I couldn't help stiffening and gasping, but Dan prodded him, "And what did Sylvia say?"

"Sylvia was a good actress. She pretended to be surprised." Then, mimicking a woman's voice, " 'Oh mercy!' she cried. 'Oh! Why, that's awful! And I'm going to have a baby! What'll I do? I haven't any money. And I'll need some right away!' Then she started to cry."

"Then what?" Dan urged.

"Then Mrs. Evers says, 'I'll give you some money. But what was it you wanted to see me about?' Sylvia stopped crying then and said, 'I wanted to warn you about —' But just then I let her see me in the doorway. Mrs. Evers was sitting at the desk writing a check and had her back to me, but Sylvia was facing me so she could see me. I was afraid she'd look scared. But like I said, she was a good actress. She said, 'I guess I don't want anything. I guess I just wanted to see you. That is — if you'll please give me some money, I'll go.' "

"And did Mrs. Evers give her money?"

"Oh, Dan," I said, "I had to. I felt so sorry for her."

Nikki said, "Shut up! I'm doing the talking." Then to Dan he said, "She gave her the check, then said she'd get her some cash. She went upstairs to get it, and while she was gone I told Sylvia I knew she'd killed Evers. She admitted it. She said he was going to leave her for another dame — not Mrs. Evers here, but a new one. She'd killed him with one of my knives so I'd be accused. She was a real little bitch sometimes. But I just laughed at her and told her I'd gotten the knife — so nobody could prove anything."

He was out of breath by that time, but Dan urged, "Go on. What else?"

"Well —" he said. He was beginning to sound very weary, and I almost expected to see the gun drop from his hand. But when he saw me glance at it, he gripped it tighter. "She said she'd tell them I did it because I was jealous. She said, 'I hate you, Nikki Radzinski, and I'm glad I never had a child for you. *Now* my baby will be a gentleman — like his father!' "

I murmured, "Poor Nikki."

But he ignored me. He didn't want sympathy at that point. He just went on talking. "She said, 'He'll be Jack Evers Junior. She —' " he nodded to me — " 'named her son after her father instead of her husband. But I'll name mine after his father. And I'll be sure they get you for his father's murder, so you won't be around to bother me.' "

I couldn't help saying, "Poor Nikki! Poor boy!"

But he snapped. "Shut up! I don't want no sympathy."

Dan continued to prod him so he'd keep talking. "Go on with your story, Nikki," he said. "Then what happened?"

Nikki ran his free hand over his head, sighed and almost forgot he was holding the gun, then remembered just in time and cocked it at my face. He began to talk again. "I guess I lost my head when she said that. I saw the paper knife on the desk, and I grabbed it and put it in her — good and deep!"

I couldn't help shivering, and I could feel Dan and Althea shudder. But Dan said, "Go on."

Nikki was showing extreme tension and utter exhaustion, and his gun hand dropped to his side. Instantly Dan was at him. He grabbed the gun from his now limp hand and backed him into a chair. Then, pointing the gun at him, Dan said, "Go on — finish your story."

Momentarily cowed, Nikki said reluctantly, "Then I ran upstairs. I could hear Mrs. Evers in the front bedroom getting the money, so I ducked into one of the back rooms. It was dark in there, and I waited until Mrs. Evers went downstairs again. Then I ran up to the top floor."

"Then what?" Dan prompted. I was beginning to wonder what would happen after

Nikki had told the entire story.

He sighed wearily. "Then I looked to see if the old dame was in her room. She was, so I told her I had the information Washington wanted, but she mustn't tell anybody I was there. Then I told her to hook the skylight after I went out and made her wrap a piece of cloth around each hand so there wouldn't be fingerprints."

"And did she?" Dan asked.

"Yes. Then she gave me a handful of those old-fashioned matches." He began to mimic Aunt Edna's voice. " 'Take them to light your way,' she said, 'but be careful. They're poison. And God be with you.' " He shook his head. "She was a nice old dame. Screwy, but nice."

He looked up at Dan and smiled wanly. "Too bad the match tips didn't kill all of you that day," he said. Then, taking Dan completely off guard, he jumped up and snatched the gun out of his hand so quickly I'm certain Dan wasn't sure how he'd done it. The next thing Dan knew, the gun was being pointed menacingly at his stomach.

Althea cried, "Dear God!" And I screamed. "Dan, look out!"

But Nikki was in command of the situation again. Glancing at Dan, he said, "Then you'd be nice and dead by now and wouldn't have to die tonight."

Dan made a tentative move toward him, and he yelled, "Put your hands up this time!"

Momentarily at a disadvantage, Dan did as he was told. Just then the front doorbell rang. The sudden sound of it brought a look of fright into Nikki's eyes. I glanced at Dan and could tell he, like myself, was hoping it was the police.

Althea said to Nikki, "That's the doorbell."

He said, "Yes, I heard it."

"Can I answer it?"

Nikki glanced menacingly at Dan. "If that's the police," he said, "so help me, I'll plug you and the dame before they can get in."

Dan said, "That would be very stupid, because then they'd have you dead to rights. Besides, if it is they, they probably have the house and the entire neighborhood surrounded so you wouldn't have a chance of getting away."

A look of panic swept over Nikki's face, and his free hand went up to his head. "Yeah, I guess you're right," he said wearily.

The bell rang again, loudly and insistently, and someone pounded on the door.

To Althea Nikki said, "Okay. Go ask who

it is. But don't open the door."

Althea ambled heavily up the two steps to the hall and over to the front door. "Who is it?" she called.

A woman's voice replied, "It's me, Althea, Mrs. Gifford. Let me in, for heaven's sakes!"

Althea turned inquiringly to Nikki. "It's Mrs. Gifford, and I'd better let her in, or she'll wake up the whole neighborhood."

Reluctantly Nikki said, "Okay, let her in. The more the merrier. I'd forgotten about her."

Althea opened the door, and Mother rushed in. Then she stopped and stared at Althea, "For heaven's sakes!" she said, "what have you got on?"

Haughtily Althea told her, "My negligee."

Mother said, "Well, it certainly is bright." Then she turned and saw the scene in the living room, with Nikki pointing the gun at Dan and me. "What on earth is going on here?" she demanded. "The sanitarium called me —"

Nikki said, "Come on down. Join the gang."

"What are you doing with that gun?" Mother demanded, not moving from the spot on which she was standing at the top of the steps to the living room.

Nikki said, "I'm getting ready to eliminate

all these nice people. And now you've ar-rived — you too."

Mother sniffed. "Don't be silly! Put that gun down!"

"No back talk!" Nikki warned her. "Get down here and stand beside your daughter there." He motioned to the place where he wanted her to stand.

"I'll do nothing of the kind!" Mother said haughtily.

"Please, Mother," I said, "he isn't kid-ding." I ventured a glance at her and saw she had just thrown her mink coat over her pa-jamas. Her hair was in a bun on top of her head and looked as if it had been fixed in a hurry. She'd stuck her bare feet into black walking shoes without any stockings.

Nikki pointed the gun at her middle. "Oh, yes, you will," he told her, "or you'll be the first to get it."

Mother hesitated, but she still held her ground. "You wouldn't dare!" she said, but this time her voice wasn't as strong as it had been before.

I said, "Please, Mother, he isn't fooling. He's desperate."

Slowly Mother came down the steps and stood beside me. "Then why doesn't some-body call the police?" she asked.

Dan said. "I have, quite a while ago. They

should be here at any minute."

"That reminds me," Nikki said. "I'd better get started. Come on back, Althea."

Reluctantly Althea returned to her place in the line-up.

Nikki pointed the gun at Dan. "You first, Brewster."

I gasped, as did Althea and Mother. Then Dan said quietly, "Just a minute. One more question — about those matches. Then it was you who put the phosphorus in the bread?"

Nikki smiled with one side of his mouth. "That's right. I got to thinking about the old dame saying the matches were poison. So I mashed up the heads and bought a loaf of bread, the kind the Evers always use. I put the powdered stuff in each slice, then put the bread back in the wrapper. And the next morning I switched my loaf for the one in Mrs. Evers' order."

"Very clever," Dan told him.

Close to tears now from the strain, I wailed, "Oh, why don't the police come?"

Sparring for still more time, Dan asked Nikki, "Anything else?"

Nikki said, "Yes. I might as well tell you. You won't be alive long enough to squeal. I read in the paper about the old dame being put in the sanitarium. So I drove up there. I was going to try to get into her room when the nurse wasn't looking. But darned if she didn't stop me on the road and thumb a ride, even before I got out to the place. It seemed like fate."

"Oh, Nikki!" I cried. "Where is she?"

"Under some bushes," Nikki told me calmly. "They'll find her this morning. I kind of hated to do away with her. She was quite a character. But I was afraid she'd talk sometime. And I couldn't keep up that Washington's aide funny business forever."

"Oh! You fiend!" Mother screamed at him, and began to cry, real tears this time.

Dan asked, "Were you here in the house a little while ago?"

Nikki said, "Yes. And I'd have finished off your girl friend here if she hadn't screamed bloody murder and waked up you and Althea."

"Where did you hide?" Dan asked him.

"I ran downstairs and got out one of those back windows, like I did one time before."

"And got back in the same way?"

"That's right."

Without moving my head, I swiveled my eyes so I could see into the back room. One of the curtains was moving almost imperceptibly. I thought, we must have left the window open. But before I could say anything, Nikki said, "Oh, by the way, I'm taking the kid to South America with me."

"Oh *no!*" I cried, feeling hysteria grip me.

Ignoring me, Nikki said, "He's a cute little feller. I like him. I'll teach him to throw knives and handle a gun."

"How did you get him?" Dan asked.

Nikki grinned. "It was easy. After I left here this afternoon, I knew that old dame —" he nodded toward Mother — "was going to come back down here. So I went to her place and got up the fire escape. Luckily, it went by the room the kid was in, all alone, watching TV. The rest was easy. We just played a game — cops and robbers. After all, I was superman." He smiled knowingly at Dan.

I gasped, and Althea grunted, which attracted his attention to us. "Come over here, you two," he said, "against the railing. Three ladies in a row — and one gentleman friend here."

I looked to Dan for help but there wasn't anything he could do. So I had to comply, with Althea reluctantly edging over beside me.

Then the front doorbell rang again, and Nikki said aloud, "Damn it to hell!"

Dan and I glanced hopefully at one another. Mother stopped crying and asked, "Who's that?"

"What do I do now?" Althea asked Nikki.

"Do like you did before. Ask who it is."

Althea lumbered up to the door again and called, "Who's there?"

From outside the door, a man said, "It's Mr. Hancock, Althea. Let me in."

Althea looked inquiringly at Nikki.

"Who is it?" Nikki asked her.

"That lawyer man."

"Oh dear!" I wailed. "Tell him to go away, Althea."

But Nikki said, "Let him in. I never did like him anyway."

So Althea opened the door, and Bryan strode in, saying, "I was driving by and saw the lights on, and I was wondering if anything was wrong?"

"Yes, sir. There's plenty wrong," Althea said, nodding to the scene in the dropped living room.

Striding to the top of the two steps, Bryan said, "Why, you gangster! Put down that gun!"

Nikki said, "Shut up! Come down here and join the rest of them. I haven't got much time left."

Bryan turned toward the front door. "I'll do nothing of the kind!" he said. "I'm going for the police!"

Nikki's gun raised over my head and fired. The bullet barely missed Bryan's left shoulder. "Oh, no, you're not," Nikki told him. "You come down here like I told you or I won't miss you next time."

Frightened now, Bryan came down into the room.

Nikki looked us all over. "Well, folks," he said, "I guess this is it. Give my love to Sylvia, if you meet her at the pearly gates. And tell her I never stopped loving her, even when I killed her."

"Just one more question," Dan said. "Was it you who phoned me to come up to your room the night I did?"

Nikki put his hand to his head. "No. Yes. I don't remember. I do things sometimes, when my head hurts, then I can't remember afterward."

Just then Bill McCarthy stepped from behind the window drapes in the back room, gun cocked, and following him were Inspector Keen, Pat, Ed and Manuel, also with guns cocked.

Nikki had his back to them and didn't see them. When Bill McCarthy said, "Okay, Nikki, the show's over!" he swung around. But before he could fire at Bill, Dan jumped him and knocked the gun from his hand. With four armed policemen in the room, and with Nikki's gun having been taken away from him, we all began to relax. As a matter of fact, I burst into tears, but they were tears of relief, "Oh, I thought you'd never get here!" I told Bill.

"We've been here for a long time," he said. "Someone was kind enough to leave one of the back windows open for us."

Nikki looked startled. Then, when he realized he'd been the one to leave the window open, he grunted something unintelligible. I rushed at him and grabbed his coat lapels, shaking him. "Where is Ronny?" I cried. "Where is my baby?"

Inspector Keen took Nikki away from me and snapped handcuffs on him. "We've got him, Mrs. Evers," he told me. "He's over at the station house, eating ice cream and having the time of his life. We found him tied up and gagged in the stolen car Nikki used to drive up to Eastchester in. It was parked on a side street near here."

"Oh, thank God!" I cried. And turning to Dan, I threw myself into his arms and began to sob. Over my shoulder Dan asked Nikki, "Did he see you dispose of Aunt Edna?"

Nikki said, "No, he was asleep. You don't think I'd let a kid see anything like that, do you?"

Pushing Nikki ahead of him, Bill said, "Okay, let's get going. These folks probably want to get some sleep."

As they went out of the door, Inspector Keen said, "The boys will bring the kid home in a little while, Mrs. Evers."

I lifted my head from Dan's shoulder. "Thank you," I said. And the four policemen, surrounding Nikki, went out.

Chapter Fifteen

Sinking into the nearest chair, Althea said, "Glory be! I'm glad it's all over!"

Then, without a sound, Mother fainted, falling in a graceful heap upon the floor. Dan, Bryan and I rushed over to her, but Althea just sat there. "Don't get excited," she said calmly. "She'll be all right. That's one of her best tricks."

At that Mother sat up, asking, "Where am I?"

"On the floor, at the moment," Dan informed her. Bryan began to help her to her feet, so Dan helped, too. But I could tell he was beginning to understand my mother and wasn't too much in sympathy with her.

Leaning against Bryan, Mother sighed deeply. "I'm too old for this kind of thing," she said petulantly.

I smoothed her hair back from her face. After all, I was all she had, and she couldn't help being the way she was. I asked, "Shall I have Dan get a taxi for you, or would you like to go upstairs and lie down?"

Sniffling, Mother said, "I don't know. I'm so upset."

Bryan said, "My car is outside. I'll drive her home."

Mother said, "Oh thank you, Bryan. That would be best."

I said, "Thanks, Bryan. If you don't mind?"

"Of course I don't mind," Bryan snapped at me. "And then I'll be back to take care of you." Then, glancing at Dan, he added, "You can't stay here any longer with this man!"

I smiled and patted his arm. "Don't worry about me, Bryan. I'll be all right. And please don't bother to come back."

Belligerently Bryan snapped, "I certainly will!"

By that time I guess Dan had about enough and no longer felt like acting like a gentleman. "If I were you," he told Bryan, "I'd do as the lady asks."

"Don't give *me* orders!" Bryan growled at him.

Mother, now perfectly recovered, pulled at Bryan's coat sleeve. "Oh, for heaven's sakes!" she said crossly, "come on, Bryan. Can't you see when you're licked?" She shoved him toward the two steps up to the hall. Then she turned and said, "Goodbye, dear," to me.

When the door had shut on Mother and

Bryan, Dan and I stood looking at each other. Then I remembered what Nikki had done to my aunt. "Poor Aunt Edna," I said. "I can't believe I'll never see her any more."

Then, to my surprise, Althea said, "Don't feel too sorry for your aunt, Miss Amelia. She wasn't as nice as you all thought she was."

I whirled on her. "What do you mean by that?" I demanded.

"What I mean is, she deliberately went after your father and deviled the life out of him. He liked her, sure; she was a very beautiful woman, in her way. But he was in love with his wife. In spite of that, Miss Edna kept after him and wanted him to get a divorce from your mother and marry her."

"I can hardly believe that," I said, shocked by her words.

"It's true," Althea told me. "Have I ever lied to you about anything?"

"Well, no," I had to admit.

"And I'm not lying to you now. It's the God's truth."

"Did my mother know?"

"Yes, she knew. That's why she hasn't been as sympathetic about Miss Edna's sickness as you thought she should be."

I looked into Althea's honest black face. "And that's why you haven't ever liked Aunt Edna?"

Althea nodded. "Yes, that's why. I knew her too well. But I didn't think you noticed I didn't like her. I took care of her, sure, since she was sick. But when she was well, she was selfish and wanted everything her own way. And she used to take all the good jobs away from your mother by hook or by crook."

I sighed. "I think I know what you mean. And in her own sweet way she always got what she wanted."

Althea nodded. "She did. And she always got what she wanted out of you, even after she got sick. And me too — I have to admit it. She had a way about her."

I guess I tried to relive my childhood in a flash to see if any of this made sense. I began to see a lot of things I hadn't noticed at the time. It made me ashamed of myself for having been so blind. "Poor Mother," I said, "I guess I've misjudged her."

"You just didn't understand," Althea said in her soft, soothing voice. "She wanted her way, too, and your poor father was torn to shreds between them."

"You felt that way about both my mother and Aunt Edna, yet you've stayed with us for all these years?"

"That's right. You can still like people even when you know their faults. They were always good to me. And I always felt like you were almost like my own child. I brought you up more than your own mother did. She was always too busy making herself beautiful."

I just stood there. I didn't know what to say. What Althea had just told me had brought the last shred of my former world tumbling down on my head.

Dan came over to me and took hold of my hands. "It's all over now. You've got to put it all behind you and make a fresh start."

I nodded, unable to speak. Then I looked up into his kindly brown eyes. Could I see a new world for me in their understanding depths? He said, "I don't have to go back to Venezuela. There's a good job here in the New York office with only an occasional inspection trip out into the field."

I smiled at him, I guess a bit ruefully. "You wouldn't be happy leading a life of domesticity," I told him.

He squeezed my hands. "I think I would. I'd like to try — with you."

I smiled then — really smiled — and in a tentative way I said, "I could sell this house. And it would be nice for Ronny out in the suburbs somewhere. But we couldn't go all alone. Besides, we've become very fond of you, Althea and Ronny and I."

Althea got to her feet and started up the

stairs. "This is no place for me," she said with a tolerant smile. "It's getting too personal."

Dan gave her a big smile. "Good night, Althea," he said.

"Good night, Mr. Dan." She leaned over the banister. "Like she said, I think you're a real nice man."

The doorbell rang, and she said, "Now who's that? I thought we were all through."

"Maybe you'd better open the door and find out," I suggested.

"In my negligee?"

I had to laugh. "You've had it on all night," I pointed out.

She grunted and started down the stairs, cautiously opening the front door.

To my relief, Ronny ran in. Manuel was with him. He said, "Here's the kid. And you don't have to worry about him. He's all right. Only I don't think he'll want any breakfast. He's too full of ice cream."

Ronny gave him his best smile. "Be seeing you," he said.

Manuel grinned and saluted. "Be seeing you," he said. Then, while Ronny was submitting to my kisses, Manuel said to Dan, "Inspector Keen said to tell you that Sylvia wasn't pregnant. They did an autopsy on her. She just wanted the money for dope, is his guess."

Dan said, "Well, thanks for telling me."

After Manuel had gone, Ronny asked, "Where's Nikki?"

"He went away," I told him.

"Where did he go?" Ronny wanted to know.

I hesitated. What could I tell him? "I don't know exactly. Why?"

"Because we were playing cops and robbers, and he tied me up and left me in a car, and then he was going to come back and rescue me, and then we were going to run away from the cops."

Tears flooded my eyes. "Did it hurt — being tied up?"

"Of course not. Nikki wouldn't hurt me. We were just playing."

I glanced at Dan, heaving a big sigh of relief. Patting Ronny's head gently, I said, "Well, all right, dear. Go on up to bed now, with Althea."

Althea came down and took his hand. "Poor little thing," she said. "Come on to bed. You're tired."

Ronny started up the stairs with Althea, but halfway up he stopped and looked over the banister at Dan. "Uncle Dan, are you going to live with us all the time?" he asked.

Dan smiled. "Yes, son, I am — eventually. Do you mind?"

"Not if you'll play baseball with me every day."

"Well, I may not be able to play every day, because I have a job. But I'll play a lot of days — and weekends."

"That'll be okay," Ronny said asking, "Have you got my ball?"

Dan said, "Yes," and Ronny let Althea lead him up to bed.

When Dan and I were alone, I said, "I overheard what Manuel told you about Sylvia."

Dan shook his head. "I guess she was really a little so and so."

I nodded agreement. "She deviled Nikki into killing her. Probably Jack knew about the drugs, and that was the reason he wouldn't give her any cash."

Dan looked tired. "Well," he said, "it's all tied up in a neat little package now."

"Is it?" I asked him. "What will they do to Nikki?"

"He may end up in the psychiatric ward of a veterans' hospital."

"You think his head wound made him do what he did?"

"That — together with Sylvia."

A sigh escaped me. "Oh dear! I really did like him."

"Maybe we can do something to help him — later."

There was nothing else to be said, so Dan just took me into his arms and kissed me. Any further plans we had to make could be made some other time.

The employees of Thorndike Press hope you have enjoyed this Large Print book. All our Large Print titles are designed for easy reading, and all our books are made to last. Other Thorndike Press Large Print books are available at your library, through selected bookstores, or directly from us.

For information about titles, please call:

(800) 223-1244
(800) 223-6121

To share your comments, please write:

Publisher
Thorndike Press
295 Kennedy Memorial Drive
Waterville, ME 04901